SECRETS

The momentum tumbled Jesse across the bitumen. Finally she stopped. She lay on her back, dizzy and disorientated. A deafening horn blared. Jesse opened her eyes to find the world was upside down. A huge, roaring monster approached. She blinked once before realizing what it was. A truck. She had rolled into its path.

Coming soon in this series

Girl Undercover 2: Fugitive
Girl Undercover 3: Nightmare
Girl Undercover 4: Danger

GIRL
UNDERCOVER

SECRETS
CHRISTINE HARRIS

■SCHOLASTIC

Scholastic Children's Books,
Euston House, 24 Eversholt Street,
London, NW1 1DB, UK
A division of Scholastic Ltd
London ~ New York ~ Toronto ~ Sydney ~ Auckland
Mexico City ~ New Delhi ~ Hong Kong

First published in Australia by Omnibus Books,
an imprint of Scholastic Australia, 2004
This edition published in the UK by Scholastic Ltd, 2006

10 digit ISBN: 0 439 95067 8
13 digit ISBN: 978 0439 95067 1

Printed by Nørhaven Paperback A/S, Denmark

10 9 8 7 6 5 4 3 2 1

Papers used by Scholastic Children's Books are made
from wood grown in sustainable forests

To Marci, an expert on spies

*Thanks to Mount Barker, Mount Barker South,
Littlehampton, and Meadows primary schools
for their enthusiastic help in the research,
and to Dyan Blacklock for a great idea.*

 **C2**

What is this organization?
Who are we working for?
What do they want from us?

Danger!

 Me

Jesse Sharpe
Who am I?
Do I have a family?
Why does C2 keep me prisoner?

Rohan

My C2 "brother".
Where is he?
Will I ever see him again?

I miss him.

Jai

My C2 "brother".
I won't escape without him.
That's a promise!

I must protect him.

Operation IQ

Secret program run by C2.

Tests, experiments on, and trains prodigies.

Why?

How can we all be orphans?

What will happen to us?

Director Granger

New head of C2.

How many secrets does he hide?

Ruthless.

Prov

Director's office manager.

Is helping me putting her in danger?

Help me!

Mary Holt

carer for IQ children.

Spies on us. Why?

Like a cobra.

Liam

My "partner".

can I trust him?

Beware!

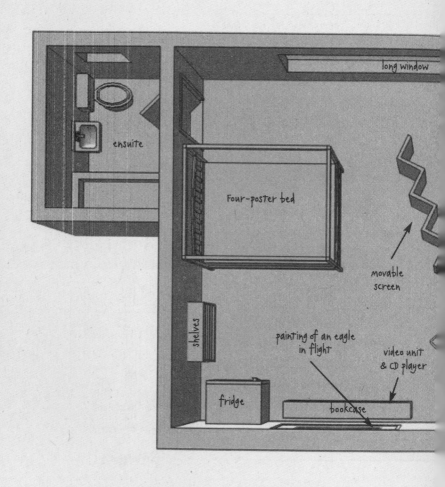

My room — "the fishbow[

long window

ensuite

Four-poster bed

movable
screen

shelves

painting of an eagle
in flight

video unit
& CD player

fridge

bookcase

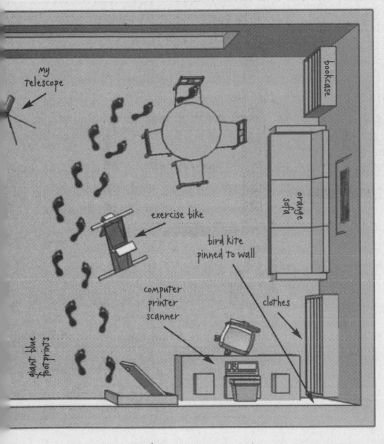

my telescope

bookcase

orange sofa

exercise bike

bird kite pinned to wall

computer printer scanner

clothes

giant blue footprints

corridor

1

A knot twisted in Jesse's stomach. Her target hadn't spotted her so far, but that could change in a second. He knew she was close. He knew she was watching him.

Without turning her head, she swivelled her eyes to the left. Passers-by would simply see a girl window shopping in the mall. Jesse checked her watch. She had to tag him in the next ten minutes.

"Got a dollar, miss?" A gruff voice rumbled into her ear. She looked up. A man with tatty dreadlocks and frayed fingerless gloves held out his hand. The flesh around his eyes was red-rimmed and crinkled. His eyeballs seemed too small for their sockets.

"Pick on someone your own size," she said and shot him a look that made him back away. She mustn't lose her target now. It was too important. If she got this right, she'd have more freedom. If not, it was back to "the fishbowl".

Again, she inspected the shifting crowd of shoppers. Yes, there he was: black trousers, grey open-necked shirt, cropped hair gelled to stand up like a miniature yellow lawn. He stopped, fingered an apple from a fruit stand, then carefully scanned the people near him.

Then he was on the move again, sauntering as though he had all the time in the world. But he didn't. Jesse smiled. He only had … oh … about eight minutes left.

Jesse loosened her hair-tie and fanned the long, blonde hair over her shoulders. She slipped off her jacket, reversed it, and put it back on. If he was looking for a glimpse of red, he would be wrong. The lining of her jacket was green. *Change something about your appearance, even if it's a little thing*, she'd learnt at training.

Casually, as though she were daydreaming, she sloped along the edge of the mall, beside the shop windows. She closed the gap between her and the man. Her fingers curled around the can in her pocket, ready to aim.

He quickened his pace and turned right into a car park.

Jesse went left, into a shoe shop opposite the car park. She turned her back and slipped on her sunglasses. The mirrored side strips allowed her to see clearly behind her.

"How may I help you?"

Jesse flicked a glance at the sales assistant, who had tight lips and thick makeup.

"What do you get if you cross a dinosaur with a pig?" asked Jesse, as she watched her target pay for his parking ticket across the mall.

"Excuse me?"

"Jurassic pork."

The assistant snorted. "Are you trying to be smart?"

I am smart, thought Jesse, but didn't say it. The sales assistant would not understand.

Across the mall, the man pressed one of the buttons outside the lift. He checked all around him. Jesse pursed her lips. *Bet he thinks he's safe. Think again, Lawnhead.*

He stepped inside the lift and the doors closed.

"Yoo hoo. Earth to space cadet." The sales assistant waved a hand in front of Jesse's face.

Jesse didn't answer. She ripped off the glasses and jammed them back into her pocket. Then she ran across the mall, the soles of her sneakers slapping against the paving bricks.

The numbers lit up above the lift – one, two, then stopped at three. Jesse opened the door to the stairs and took them two at a time. She began to puff and her chest hurt. By the second flight of stairs, her legs were screaming at her to stop. *Floor two … three.* This was it.

She edged open the door, just a crack. It made only the slightest of sounds as the latch clicked back. *There he is, digging in his pocket for keys.* Two minutes to go, maybe three.

After a couple of deep breaths, she dropped to the ground, squeezed around the partly open door and let it close quietly. Crab-like, she scuttled across the oil-stained floor and around cars. She pressed her body flat, peering underneath the car beside her. Two legs, covered by black trousers, stood on the other side. His shoes were scuffed at the front.

On a lower level, car tyres squealed as someone gunned the engine.

Suddenly the lift pinged. Jesse heard the doors open, then voices. The man's feet spun round so he could face the lift. She knew, without looking, that his hand would be inside his jacket pocket. His heart, like hers, would be pounding and he would be ready to lunge.

Children's voices, high and irritated, echoed off the walls.

A deeper, older voice snapped back, "Be quiet or I'll take the toys back."

The man's feet did not move. He stood rock-still, ready for anything. Was he wondering if this woman with the arguing children was his hunter?

Jesse grabbed the can from her pocket. *Now! Get him*

while he's distracted. She leapt to her feet. Instinctively, he half-turned. But he was too slow. Jesse squeezed the nozzle and blasted the man in the face. A similar can dropped from his fingers on to the cement with a *clack*, then rolled away. The man crumpled, unconscious. His head met the concrete with a thud.

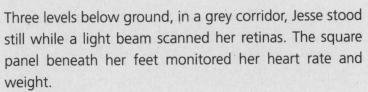

Three levels below ground, in a grey corridor, Jesse stood still while a light beam scanned her retinas. The square panel beneath her feet monitored her heart rate and weight.

"Jesse Sharpe, you are cleared for entry," came an electronic voice from a hidden speaker.

Behind her, two bulky guards, muscled arms folded, stood on each side of the underground corridor. The doors slid open silently. She stepped from the corridor into the Director's waiting room.

His office manager, Prov, sat behind her broad, oak desk. She wore a yellow, fluffy jumper. Her black hair was teased high and her brown eyes rimmed by eyeliner. Red sculptured nails made her fingers look extra long. Jesse didn't know how she could type with those nails.

A warm smile lit up Prov's face. "Jesse!"

Jesse smiled back. She couldn't help it. Prov's smile was like a fire on a cold day.

Prov beckoned Jesse to her desk and whispered, "I have something for you."

Within a few seconds, a bite-sized Mars bar was whisked from Prov's handbag to Jesse's hand, and into her mouth. The chocolate flavour burst on her tongue as she bit down. *Mmm.* She wasn't allowed junk food. "Healthy body, healthy mind," her carer, Mary Holt, always said. Well, Mary didn't know everything. This organization dealt in secrets. Chocolate was just another one. Prov glanced over her shoulder at the closed door. "I think Director Granger's in a good mood. As far as I can tell, anyway."

Prov said he refused to use the shortened version of her name. He insisted on calling her Providenza. It was Italian for *providence* – the protective care of God or nature. Her mother had almost lost Prov when she was pregnant, so the doctors packed her in ice for four months. The baby – Prov – was born with pneumonia. Yet she lived.

The new Director of C2 was hard to read. Jesse had only met him once, when he gave her the test assignment. There were whispers that he intended to make changes. Whether they would be good or bad, she didn't know.

Prov raised one eyebrow. "He's got someone in there with him."

Jesse wished this appointment was over. Then she would know what was going to happen. She had tagged the big, blond man within the time-limit. That was good. But what if he had been seriously injured from the bump on his head? That would be bad. Jesse wiped her moist palms on her jeans.

She thought of Rohan, her C2 "brother". Where was he now? "He was sick," was all they told her. "He went to a place where doctors heal the mind." Rohan had not seemed sick to her. But he had asked a lot of questions. He'd dropped hints about hacking into C2's computers. Even at eleven, he knew more about computers than most people would learn in their entire lives. Then Rohan was gone.

"Jesse."

She jumped. *Granger!* She hadn't heard his office door open.

Behind his back, Prov gave Jesse the thumbs-up sign and mouthed the words, *Go girl.* But there was an extra worry-line between her eyes.

Jesse stood and entered Granger's spacious office. Because it was underground, there were no windows, just framed maps on the walls.

A man stood in the centre of the room. He was

8

dressed in black trousers, grey shirt, and his blond hair stuck up like a newly mown lawn. A feeling of dread spread through Jesse as she recognized him. He turned. A bruised lump stood out from his brow.

The door snapped shut behind her.

Jesse stared at the man she had tagged in the car park.

His eyebrows rose. He looked from Jesse to the Director, and back again.

He doesn't know who I am. She had knocked him out with the spray before he had seen her. Besides, she looked a lot different now. Jesse sighed. She'd been holding her breath without realizing it.

"Take a chair, Jesse." Director Granger walked to his desk and sat behind it. "You too, Liam."

Jesse chose the seat closest to the door. She sneaked a look at the lump on Liam's forehead. *Ouch. That had to hurt.* He didn't have a face that would win prizes anyway. Liam's nose was wide, unusually flat and leant to the left. His yellowish skin was pockmarked. The expression on his face would sour milk.

"Liam," said the Director. "Meet your hunter."

Liam turned towards the door, but it remained shut.

Director Granger said nothing. Neither did Jesse. Every second seemed etched into the air. Then Liam's gaze settled on Jesse. A strange look entered his eyes. "*No.*"

The Director nodded and pressed his long, white fingers together.

"I was tagged by a *kid*?"

Liam said *kid* as though it were a disease. Jesse felt less guilty about the lump on his head.

"I don't believe it." He turned in his chair for a better look at her.

"I was wearing a wig," said Jesse. Long blonde hair and green contacts had changed her appearance. Now, she knew Liam would see light brown hair, cropped short, and brown eyes.

"Don't feel too bad, Liam," said the Director. "Jesse is a prodigy, a genius. Like the famous William Sidis, she read encyclopedias at three years of age. She speaks five languages and learnt to play clarinet in one day. Her memory is remarkable. We put her with a surveillance expert for two hours and she followed you without detection."

Liam did not look impressed.

"Jesse is part of Operation IQ," added Director Granger.

She sat silently, but her mind was whirring. C2 was riddled with code names, not just Operation IQ.

Everything had a hidden side. It was a world of shadows. Sometimes she found it hard to tell what was real.

Director Granger smoothed down his green silk tie with one hand. "If we can discover what makes child geniuses, we can encourage our own. If we learn what they're capable of ... well, it's an important contribution to science."

A contribution to science? Jesse's mind erupted with questions that she dared not ask out loud. She felt like a starving person being fed grains of rice one at a time.

Liam fingered the lump on his head.

"I'm sorry you were hurt," she said. "I didn't mean..."

Director Granger cut across her apology. "You were following orders, Jesse. Tag and run."

"You should have told me you'd sent a kid." Liam sent her a withering stare. "I was looking for someone who didn't suck her thumb."

"I have never sucked my thumb," said Jesse in a calm voice that hid the churning of her stomach. "It ruins the arch of a person's upper teeth." She pointed to his untidy thatch of hair. "Is that a wig too?"

The way his lips pressed into an angry line told her that it wasn't. That figured. If he had a choice of disguise, he wouldn't have picked that one.

"Liam, despite your hurt pride, Jesse did well today.

In one hour, she had you tagged and unconscious. Not bad for someone who, until now, has been nurtured, kept separate from the annoying trifles of life."

Nurture? In her mind, Jesse saw a dictionary definition of the word. It meant *fostering care*. Is that how the Director described years of questions and uncomfortable experiments in the laboratory?

She felt more like an animal in a zoo – stared at, prodded, examined and spoken to without anyone really knowing the Jesse that was more than her quick mind. Once she had tried to run away, to escape into that noisy world outside, full of other children and toys and chocolate shops. But only once. What happened afterwards gave her nightmares.

4

Director Granger tapped his fingertips together. "No one sees children, Liam. They're often overlooked. That's what we need. Someone who is watching, listening, but doesn't stand out."

Jesse felt a prickling at the back of her neck. Did this mean she had passed the test, that he would give her more freedom?

"Liam. Meet your new partner."

"What?" Liam leapt to his feet. "You can't send me out with *her!*"

"Yes, I can. And I am. A situation has come up and Jesse is the perfect choice to help us." There was an expression in Granger's narrowed eyes that made her think of black, slimy mould. Despite his fancy suit and formal manners, he was dangerous.

Liam might have thought so too because he didn't argue further.

"Jesse, I am sending you out with Liam on a field assignment."

She exchanged looks with Liam. Neither of them smiled. He was grumpy and rude, but also her means of discovering the outside world for herself.

"But a warning for you, Jesse. Never let down your guard. Remain alert. Suspect everyone." Director Granger opened a drawer in his desk and pulled out a large photograph. He held it out to Jesse.

Her fingers trembled slightly as she took it. There she was, in the long, blonde wig, talking to a beggar with dreadlocks and fingerless gloves in the mall. She remembered his gruff voice. "Got a dollar, miss?"

"He's one of our field agents," said the Director. "You were tagged."

She had been so busy looking ahead that she had not checked behind.

Director Granger shook his head. "If that was a real situation, you'd be dead."

Jesse opened the door to her room on the tenth floor of the C2 building.

Mary Holt, her carer, was bent forward, arms outstretched, searching under Jesse's mattress. At the sound of the door, Mary jumped and dropped the mattress back into place. Her cheeks flushed red. She opened her eyes wide as if to say, *You can trust me.*

Yeah right, thought Jesse, *and I'm a Martian.* "All you'll find under there are snotty tissues," said Jesse. She walked across to stand in front of the large windows.

"I was checking if your bed needed stripping."

"Sheets are usually on *top* of the mattress."

"I thought the mattress might be musty." As Mary recovered from her surprise, the red on her cheeks faded to pink. Jesse knew it was not the first time Mary had searched her room. Although she was not usually clumsy enough to get caught.

Sometimes it was only a small object out of place that revealed Mary's snooping. Jesse's excellent memory gave her an advantage. She knew exactly where she had left everything.

At least her computer was safe. She had set it up with fingerprint recognition and changed her four passwords every day. Even her screensaver had a password. If anyone but her broke through a gateway, the whole system would shut down and eat the files. She sometimes wondered if someone from C2 would confiscate her computer, but so far it hadn't happened.

Mary dusted her hands and pushed her frizzy hair back from her face. "Atlantic salmon for tea tonight, and organically grown vegetables. Fish has omega 3. It's good brain food."

Jesse wished that one day Mary would offer a hamburger. But it would never happen.

"How do you know it's been to the Atlantic?" asked Jesse. She imagined a large fish with a sticker on its back – *I've been to the Atlantic.*

"That's just the name of it." Mary looked at Jesse suspiciously. "Is that a joke?"

Jesse shrugged.

"I'd better get going. Busy. Busy." Mary moved towards the door like a cobra about to strike. She pushed her head forward with every step, as though she wanted her face to get somewhere before her feet. As usual, she left Jesse's door open. To her, privacy was only another word in the dictionary. Still, it didn't matter this afternoon. It was almost time for Jai to arrive.

Jesse adjusted her telescope and examined the passers-by, ten floors below. She liked watching families: parents with prams; children with pets.

She zoomed in on a mother and daughter. The girl was about Jesse's age. Mother and daughter were dressed alike, with faded blue jeans and T-shirts. Even their hair was cut in a similar way. The mother rested one hand gently on the girl's head. Jesse looked away. She could never be that girl.

Soon the lights would come on, Jesse's favourite time. Then she couldn't see the littered streets or grimy buildings. The city would sparkle.

Tomorrow I'll be out there in the real world. Excitement rushed through her. For a little while, she would be free from this room she called "the fishbowl". She sometimes thought of herself as a goldfish, trapped behind glass, staring out. But it was dangerous outside. Her partner, Liam, already disliked her and called her a "thumb sucker". What if this assignment went wrong and she didn't come back? Then a scarier thought hit her. What if it was a trap to get rid of her? Is that what happened to Rohan?

6

I won't think about it. If Jesse was too scared, she couldn't think clearly. And like a tightrope walker with no safety net, she needed to concentrate to stay alive.

She looked up at the wall clock, with its back-to-front numbers. A Christmas present from Prov. Jai would arrive precisely on time. She could set her clock by his routines. Her C2 "brothers" were opposites in that way. Rohan had little idea of time. Jai was obsessed by it.

As though her thought had conjured him up, Jai entered the room. They had shaved his head again. The regrowth looked like a brown stain. He lifted his violin to his left shoulder. Eyes closed, his small fingers delicately holding the bow, he began to play one of his own compositions.

Some people said he made the violin talk. Jesse disagreed. It was more than that. He made it *feel*. It laughed, cried and teased. This piece made her think of water dancing down rocks and, finally, swelling into a deep pool. He finished on a long, soft note that drifted into silence.

Jai opened his eyes. His voice was soft and high-pitched. As always, he spoke in a formal way, no clipped sentences, no slang. "How would you improve this piece of music?"

"Stop playing it," said Jesse dryly.

"For a child prodigy, your jokes are quite bad."

"Mary doesn't think I tell any."

"Mary does not think," he said. "She only obeys."

"I can't be perfect at everything."

"Why not?" Jai tilted his head to one side.

"Then I'd be a pain and no one would like me."

"Who likes you now?"

"You do."

He smiled. Then, stepping carefully, he followed the massive blue footprints Jesse had cut out of cardboard and stuck to the carpet. They led across the room and around her circular wooden table. The last print was on a chair. As he did most nights, Jai climbed on to the chair, stood in the centre of the last cardboard footstep and took a bow.

Jesse closed her door.

Jai climbed down and carefully placed the violin and bow on the table. "Did you know that the mother of

Janos Starker, the celloist, made tiny sandwiches and left them on his music stand so that he would not have to stop practice to eat?"

"That's cute."

Jai took a small metal tube the size of a biro from his left pocket and scanned underneath the table and chairs.

"She also trained a parrot to say *Practise, Janos, practise.*"

"Not so cute."

Jai scanned the bookcases, four-poster bed, fridge, video unit, and the large painting of an eagle soaring over a high mountain.

Jesse watched silently.

Then he checked the computer desk, the exercise bike, her clothes hanging from a metal rail, the orange sofa, and the massive bird kite pinned to the wall.

"There are no listening devices today." Every time Jai found one, he had an "accident" with it. It would fall under his foot or drop into the toilet bowl.

Jai returned the scanner to his pocket and patted it.

A small silence stretched into awkwardness.

Jesse struggled to think of what to say. Usually they had no problem talking to each other. However, so much had happened in the last couple of days and she could not tell Jai any of it.

21

"Did you hear about the two cannibals who ate a clown?" she said. "One said to the other, *Does this taste funny to you?*"

Jai aimed a penetrating stare at Jesse. "What are you hiding?"

7

Jesse laughed too loudly. "What makes you think I'm hiding something?" How could she explain that she was going outside, while Jai remained here?

"I am a genius."

"So am I," she said.

"Yes, but you are not as clever as I."

Jesse did not argue. "I ... I can't tell you." Earlier, Director Granger had fixed his iceberg eyes on her and demanded total secrecy. Besides, if this was a trap, information could put Jai in danger. Jesse had to keep him out of it.

The look in Jai's eyes reminded her of the labrador she had seen on one of her guarded "test runs" outside. It had been hit by a car and lay injured in the gutter. The dog's eyes had pleaded for help.

"Jai. You're the closest thing to family that I have. We're like brother and sister. I want to tell you, but ...

I *can't*. You might be in danger."

"Look where we live. I am always in danger."

Jesse nodded. "This could be worse."

"You are going outside."

She nodded. "But I'll be back." Even though the words came from her own mouth, she felt reassured when she heard them.

"It is now six-thirty p.m. on your foolish clock. We must begin our Yahtzee game." Jai tugged at his fringe. Any change in routine worried him, especially if he was upset.

Jesse opened a drawer in the video cabinet and took out a score pad, pen and five green dice. Jai couldn't handle playing with dice of different colours. It didn't matter *which* colour, but they all had to be the same.

They sat at the table.

Jai pressed his palms flat to the surface. "Why do you use a score pad? We will both remember the sequence of numbers."

"I don't want to argue with you about the scores. You like to win."

"As do you."

"I like to compete. Winning is extra. Your turn to start." Jesse pushed the dice across the table. "Have you beaten your computer at chess yet?"

"No. But I programmed it, so I still win." Jai rolled the dice three times. "Yahtzee."

Jesse wrote down his score, then had her turn.

Jai pursed his lips. "The statistical probability of your attaining a high straight at this point is poor."

"Sometimes you have to take a risk."

"Jesse." Jai cleared his throat. "Do not take too many risks … out there, will you?"

"I won't," she said.

But she didn't believe it. Nor did he.

Goosebumps dotted Jesse's skin. Anything could happen today. She lengthened her steps. Keeping up with Liam was like chasing a tree blown along by a typhoon. He turned right, following the tunnel. Jesse stayed close behind him.

No one who worked for C2 left by the usual doors. They took tunnels to a secret car park. People who came and went through the front doors were real customers seeking insurance. They had no idea that Trust Insurance Company covered a more secret business.

Liam stopped suddenly and Jesse almost ran into the back of him. He ignored her. *Do I care?* she thought, then decided she did. A few kind words would have helped a lot this morning. But she would never admit it.

He stopped at a set of lift doors and placed his palm against the identification scanner. No one passed in or out without C2 authorization.

"What's that supposed to be?" Liam glanced sideways.

"A backpack. For school."

"Give it here."

Reluctantly she handed it over, then followed him into the lift.

Liam dropped the backpack. Then he raised one foot and stomped on it, scraping his boot backwards and forwards.

Jesse gasped. "What are you doing?"

He flipped the backpack over with the toe of his boot and scraped the other side. "It's too clean and new-looking. You'll look like a loser. You're supposed to blend in." He inspected the scuff marks and nodded. "That's better. Now it looks like a normal kid's bag."

Smothering disappointment, Jesse snatched her backpack. It looked as though a herd of wild animals had trampled over it. She glared at Liam. Well, maybe not a herd. Just one.

He took a long look at her neat, brushed hair.

"Don't even think about it," she said. "I have a black belt in tae kwon do." He still had a bruise on his forehead from his fall in the car park. If he touched her hair, he'd have another one.

Liam's scowl lightened. Was he going to smile? That'd be a first. "So do I, as a matter of fact."

The lift halted and the doors opened. Liam held out

27

one arm as he peered left and right. "Looks OK."

His car was parked close by. She had hoped for a red sports car with ejector seats and buttons that fired missiles. But Liam's car had spots of rust and a dented bumper bar.

She saw her reflection in the side mirror. Her school uniform of navy track pants and white T-shirt were comfortable, but boring.

Inside the car, she kicked paper and cardboard containers aside. Liam ate a lot of takeaways.

The car matches his hair. Today he had gone easy on the gel. His blond hair pointed wherever it liked. He wore overalls that were too short, leaving a gap above his socks, with a hint of hairy legs.

Jesse stretched the seatbelt across her body and locked it.

Liam turned the ignition key.

Jesse sneaked a look at him. His lips were pressed together in a grim line. She wished he would say something. *Anything*. Her first assignment outside, and she was with a zombie. It walked, it moved its eyes, but it didn't speak.

She placed the scuffed backpack at her feet.

Back in the tunnel, Liam had said that the school kids might think she was a loser. Is that what *he* thought?

She took a deep breath. "You think I'm a freak, don't you?'

28

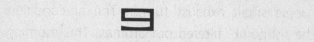

9

"We're all freaks." Liam shrugged. "Otherwise, why would we work for an organization like C2?"

"I don't work for them," said Jesse. "They adopted me."

"What happened to your parents?"

"There was a car accident. My parents were killed but I survived. I was one year old."

"You don't have other relatives?"

Liam's voice had an edge of doubt, and it disturbed her. It was a question she had often wondered herself.

"I don't think so," said Jesse. "I don't know anything about my family."

"So, who is this William Sidis that Granger mentioned?"

She stared through the window as they drove out of the car park, not wanting to miss a thing. "William Sidis read books when he was two. At six, he spoke Hebrew, German, Greek, French, Russian and English. He wrote four books between the ages of four and eight. And when he was eleven, he went to Harvard University."

"Bit slow, was he?" Liam braked and put on the right indicator.

Jesse smelt exhaust fumes. The air-conditioning in "the fishbowl" filtered out aromas. This morning there were dozens of smells to identify: coffee, toast, stale chips, and a touch of something spicy. Liam's deodorant or aftershave, maybe.

"Humans can distinguish 10,000 different aromas," said Jesse.

Liam sniffed.

OK, thought Jesse, *so you can also use your nose to say, Who cares?* She was tempted to stir him even further by adding, *If your nose runs and your feet smell, then you're upside down,* but she didn't think he'd find it funny.

"Do you understand what your job is?" asked Liam.

"Yes."

"You cover the school and I'll do the house. I've got a position as a groundsman. Make friends with the target. Get as close as you can."

Without taking his eyes from the road, he slipped his left hand into his pocket and took out a watch. "Here. Take this."

"I've got a watch," said Jesse. This one Liam offered

was chunky, more like a man's watch.

He dropped it into her lap. "There's more to it than meets the eye. If you press the alarm set button, it changes the face. You can use it to send me a message."

She swapped it for her own watch, slipping hers into an outside zip-up pocket of the backpack.

"Contact me if you need help. But make the messages short. If someone is looking for you, they can triangulate where you are by reading the signal. But you'll be OK if you're brief."

Oh great. Contact me if you're in trouble, but the enemy might find you if you do.

"My contact number is already recorded there. It's easy to use. Especially for a mega-brain like you. And be careful out there. Watch your back."

She had learnt that from her encounter with the dreadlocked man in the mall.

"At this stage, we don't know how to tell the good guys from the bad. And even good guys can be as ruthless as the bad."

"Wouldn't being ruthless make you one of the bad guys?"

Liam's hands gripped the steering wheel tightly. His knuckles stood out. "Nothing is that simple, especially with this kind of work. We infiltrate. We seek information. We obey orders. Full stop. Do yourself a favour and don't try to work it all out. Just do your part and forget the rest."

But what if those orders included something she didn't want to do, something that might hurt someone?

"Last year a friend of mine, interstate, worked with a kid from Operation IQ," added Liam. "This kid went nuts, turned into a whacko who stayed in his room, making models out of lollypop sticks. Don't go nuts on me, will you? You could get us both killed."

Jesse's heart pounded in her ears. She turned her face away from Liam, hiding her confusion. *A kid from Operation IQ? Interstate?* All this time she thought there were just the three of them, her, Jai and Rohan. But there were others. What did this mean?

Her head spun. Terrorists worked in what they called "cells'. Most of the cells or groups didn't know about the others. If someone from one cell was captured, he could not give information about the others. Is that how it was with Operation IQ? But why?

10

Thirty faces stared at Jesse. She had never been with so many other kids. They all wore similar navy track pants and white T-shirts. It was like being in a room full of clones, except the faces were different. There were paintings of fish and a poster of an Egyptian pyramid pinned on the classroom walls. A musty odour hung in the air. A boy in the front row shifted his feet and the smell became stronger. Was it his sneakers?

"Class, we have a new person joining us today. Jesse Sharpe. Let's welcome her." The teacher, Mr Rathbone, clapped his hands. Most kids joined him. A few looked bored. The boy with the smelly sneakers rolled his eyes.

Mentally, Jesse checked each face in the room against the class photo she had been shown at C2. Someone was missing.

"Excuse me, sir." The kid with smelly feet put up his hand. "There's something wrong with my finger."

"What, Hugh?" barked Mr Rathbone.

"It keeps going up my nose!" The boy snorted loudly through both nostrils. He looked around to see how many of his classmates thought he was funny.

The teacher sent him a glare that would wither stone.

"Excuse our bad manners, Jesse." Mr Rathbone smiled at her, revealing the unusually pale gums of dentures. He had a large head that bobbed up and down as he spoke. He was bald on top with the side hair cut short. It looked as though a horseshoe curled around his skull. "Tell us a little about yourself."

A screwed-up ball of paper flew through the air and hit Hugh on the back of the head. He twisted around to see who had thrown it.

Jesse cleared her throat. "I live with a carer. A nanny. Whatever you want to call her."

Several girls sat up straighter and looked at her more carefully.

"My parents are overseas. They work in a circus, looking after the elephants. Mum polishes their toenails and Dad's a vet. He's especially interested in teeth. Elephants" teeth are as big as house bricks. If an elephant's teeth wear down too far, it can't eat and it dies."

Doubt sat like a *For Sale* sign on Mr Rathbone's face.

A ripple of whispers circled the room.

The door opened suddenly. A girl bolted inside in a flurry of arms and legs. Strands of hair like tiny tentacles framed her face. "Sorry I'm late, Mr Rathbone." She held up a small black case. "Flute lesson went overtime."

Long brown hair, blue eyes, a tiny scar above the right eyebrow, and a small mouth.

Yes. This is Jasmine Carrillo, the girl in the photo. The one who's going to be kidnapped.

11

Beside the oval, Jesse sat with her back against a wall. From there she could see most of the school grounds, yet no one could sneak up behind her. How long would it take Jasmine to find her?

Jesse took a bite of the fruit cake Mary had prepared for her recess. Even though Jesse chewed it well, it still felt like lumps sliding down her throat. It would have organically grown wholemeal flour, free range eggs and no sugar. Jesse wouldn't put it past Mary to slip in some bran.

The sunshine warmed Jesse's face. She watched the boys play football. They seemed to get more fun out of tugging each other's shirts and tackling each other to the ground than handling the ball.

To her right, a small figure broke away from a group and headed towards her. Every nerve was alert. She wanted to appear relaxed, but she needed to be ready for anything. Jesse didn't look up. She didn't want to seem too eager.

A shadow moved across Jesse's outstretched legs.

"Hi." Jasmine sat beside Jesse, a paperback book and a plump paper bag on her lap. "Is it true that your parents look after elephants?"

Jesse nodded.

"I *love* elephants." Jasmine's blue eyes sparkled.

"Really?" Jesse pretended surprise. She knew a lot of things about Jasmine. "Elephants have feet like Nike Airs, you know. They're kind of spongy. Their feet squash out when they step on the ground, then shrink when they lift them back up. That's why they don't get stuck in the mud."

"Cool." Jasmine opened the paper bag and took out a chocolate doughnut.

Jesse stared at it, saliva pooling on her tongue.

"Want some?" Jasmine broke the doughnut and offered half to Jesse.

I have to take it to be friendly. Liam would tell me to eat it, I know he would. Jesse bit into the piece of doughnut with anticipation. It was even better than she had imagined.

"What have you got?" Jasmine pointed to the fruit cake.

"A brick."

37

Jasmine laughed. "Let me try it." She broke off a corner of fruit cake with two fingers. She chewed. And chewed. Then swallowed as if she hadn't chewed at all. "Definitely a brick."

The two girls exchanged grins.

Get close to her, Liam had said. *Become her best friend, her shadow.*

The football soared in their direction then bounced off the wall. Jesse and Jasmine ducked. Two boys thundered after the ball. One of them was Hugh with the smelly sneakers.

"They did that on purpose," said Jasmine. "Because we were here."

"But they didn't even look at us."

Jasmine nodded. "That's how I know they did it on purpose." She wiped her sticky fingers on the paper bag.

Jesse blinked. *I've got a lot to learn about people. I know more about elephants. And there aren't going to be many of those around here.* Although she had noticed the principal was overweight and wore a grey suit.

"Have you seen a real elephant?" asked Jasmine.

Jesse considered making up another story but decided against it. "No, only photos. My parents think it's a better life for me here. They're always travelling to different places and they live in a caravan. I don't want to live in a caravan anyway."

"Me neither."

"I've seen lots of photos of elephants," added Jesse. "My parents sometimes email them to me. I had one from them a week ago when they were in Bangkok. This elephant had a reflector light on its tail, like a car, and its head was inside a nightclub doorway. All you could see was this fat elephant bottom sticking out of the door, swaying to the music." It was only half made up. She had seen the photo on the Internet.

"How do you know if there's an elephant under your bed?" asked Jesse.

"I don't know."

"Your nose scrapes the ceiling."

Jasmine chuckled. "I have a book of elephant pictures, and an elephant quilt cover. And I have a collection of elephant statues. Some of them are really small, but I've got sixty-seven. I might stop when I get to a hundred. But maybe not. You should come over and see them some time."

"Sure." Jesse tried to sound casual, but she *had* to visit Jasmine's house.

Jesse looked at the oval, then the playground. There were just kids fighting, eating and playing. And a couple of teachers trying to ignore them.

Jasmine scrunched up the paper bag tightly in her palm. Jesse turned at the sound.

Over Jasmine's shoulder, she saw a white van parked across the street. A man in overalls sat on a fold-up stool. His dark hair hung down under his broad-brimmed hat to touch his shoulders. A junction-box door was open and the wires were exposed. *Power or phone company?* Yet something about him was odd. What was it?

She focused carefully, paying special attention. The man didn't seem to be doing any work. He was staring right in their direction.

12

Jasmine opened her book. "My oral review is due after recess. I haven't read it so I'm just going to look at the last page of each chapter. That should tell me what happens. I *hope*."

A flash of light drew Jesse's attention back to the man in the overalls. The sun glinted off something small that he held up to his right eye. *That's a magnifier.*

If this man was in on the plan to kidnap Jasmine, would he take her from school? Wouldn't it be easier to catch her on her way home? Or couldn't they wait? Jesse felt frustrated. She didn't even know who "they" were. All Granger had told her was that they were enemies of Jasmine's father.

The man across the street turned slightly. His lips appeared to be moving.

Jesse unzipped her track pants pocket, took out a tissue and pretended to blow her nose. Then she brushed an invisible hair back from her face. As she did so, she slipped a tiny listening device called a spy ear from her palm into her left ear and pressed it.

Instantly, the playground noises were exaggerated, deafening. She tapped the spy ear to turn it off. Her head still rang with the boom, crash, squeal of the schoolyard.

She had to get closer to the man, away from these other sounds. "I'll be back in a minute," she told Jasmine.

Jasmine nodded and kept turning the pages of her book. Jesse walked to the girls" toilets, entered the cubicle nearest the road and quickly locked the door. She lifted the plastic seat, then stood on the porcelain bowl. Her head was level with the frosted louvre window. Someone had scribbled on the wall, *Eat prunes and get a run for your money.* She tapped the spy ear. *That's better.*

A male voice, faint but audible, came from across the street. "Yes, sir ... both here. I can see them from my position ... Pardon? You'll have to speak up. I'm sure ... one of them has gone to the loo ... no problem."

Jesse was tempted to leap down and hide. It was as though he could see her perched there like a bird on an aerial. *Don't panic. Even with the best magnifier, he can't see through brick walls.*

"Neither of them has left the school. Being good little girls, they are."

42

Jesse ground her teeth. The way he said "good little girls" sounded like an insult. She wanted to take that cute little phrase and wrap it around his head.

"No, sir … they have no idea."

That's what you think.

"She's sticking with the other girl so far … If I see that, I'll let you know."

See what? Hearing one side of the conversation was worse than hearing none. *There's no way this peanut is getting his hands on Jasmine.*

"Yes, sir. I understand. Watch Sharpe."

Jesse gasped. *Sharpe* wasn't Jasmine's surname. It was hers.

13

After school, Jesse watched as Jasmine squeezed through the school gate. Her overloaded backpack bounced off a post.

There was no sign of the long-haired man who knew her name, or his van. Who was he? Another C2 agent checking on her? Or had the people who threatened Jasmine discovered who had sent Jesse? But how could they have found out so quickly?

Jesse called out, "Hey, Jasmine!"

She turned.

"I think this might be yours." Jesse held out a calculator.

Jasmine turned it over to check the initials on the back – *JC*. "Thanks. I didn't realise I'd dropped it."

"That's OK." It had taken Jesse only a second to slip it from Jasmine's backpack when she wasn't looking.

"You going this way too?"

Jesse nodded.

"Let's walk together."

"Great idea."

Jesse kept a keen lookout for the man with long hair or anyone else who might seem suspicious. Why was Jasmine walking home alone if she was in danger? Hadn't Director Granger warned her family? They might not want to scare Jasmine, but wouldn't it be better to be scared than kidnapped? *Typical. Can anyone at C2 even walk in a straight line?*

A maroon car cruising too slowly caught Jesse's attention. The driver wore a hat and dark glasses. A man, judging by the broad shoulders. The number plate of his car was covered in mud, unreadable.

It could just be someone looking for a parking spot or a house number.

Just in case, Jesse swapped sides with Jasmine to walk nearest the curb. That way, someone in a car would have to get past her to grab Jasmine.

"I have to walk near the road or I feel all squashed," said Jesse. "Weird, isn't it?"

"Maybe. But I make all my shoes face the same way in the wardrobe – so I can't talk about weird."

Hot pins and needles shot through Jesse when she heard the word "wardrobe'. They were dark places where things were locked in, kept away from the light. Her bedroom only had a long rail from which to hang clothes. She would never, *ever* have a wardrobe.

The driver of the maroon car accelerated and turned a corner. Jesse relaxed a little. He must have been looking for a particular street.

She followed Jasmine past busy shops and cafes. *So much noise.* Jesse couldn't hear anything like this from her room ten floors up. Car horns, the *va voom, va voom* of a CD player that was turned up too loud, a dog barking and human voices that faded in and out as they passed other pedestrians. It was exciting and confusing. *What would Jai think about all these colours?* Most things in his room were either black or white.

"So what's the woman who looks after you like?" asked Jasmine.

"Think of the fruit cake."

"You said it was a brick."

"Yeah." Jesse smirked.

Jasmine smirked right back at her. "We're going to be best friends, I can tell."

A warm glow fired inside Jesse. No one had ever said that to her before. Not just a friend, but a *best* friend. All she had to do was keep Jasmine alive.

14

Jesse caught a flash of maroon reflected in a department store window. The muddied car was back. Her instinct kicked into action. *I have to get Jasmine off this street – now.*

"How many seconds do you think it would take us to run from this end of the shop through to the other?" Jesse grabbed Jasmine's arm.

"I don't know…"

"Thirty?"

Jasmine bolted. As the double glass doors slid open, she disappeared inside the store. Jesse gasped, then chased after her. Jasmine had reacted faster than she'd expected.

Jesse's backpack thumped against her spine as she ran. Her feet made little sound on the carpet. Left and right, directly behind her new friend, Jesse darted around customers. Faces were a blur of raised eyebrows and O-shaped mouths. *Oops – a pram.* Jesse leapt sideways, then continued towards the back doors.

Running gave her a sense of being free and wild. Her legs pumped like motor pistons. Her hair whipped her face.

Jasmine stopped abruptly. The automatic doors were too slow. She almost collided with the glass. Jesse ran into Jasmine's backpack. *Oofph.* They both squealed, then shot through the open doors like two bullets fired from a gun.

Outside, Jasmine bent double, gasping for air. "Forgot … to check … the time we…" She took a deep breath. "Started."

"Me too."

Jasmine giggled.

"Which way is your place?" asked Jesse.

Jasmine pointed, without speaking.

After a quick check over her shoulder, Jesse followed Jasmine down a narrow lane and out on to another street.

In the short wait for the pedestrian light to turn green, Jesse took a few deep breaths. Her legs stopped trembling.

They were halfway across the street when Jesse heard the roar of a motor, then the screech of tyres. To her left, a maroon car shot straight towards them. The driver hunched down, both hands gripping the steering wheel.

"Look out!" she shouted at Jasmine.

Jasmine hesitated.

The maroon car closed in. In only a few seconds, it would smash into them.

Jesse dropped her bag, leapt forward and shoved Jasmine in the back. Jasmine flew forward.

The momentum tumbled Jesse across the bitumen. Finally she stopped. She lay on her back, dizzy and disorientated. A deafening horn blared. Jesse opened her eyes to find the world was upside down. A huge, roaring monster approached. She blinked once before realizing what it was. A truck. She had rolled into its path.

15

There was no time to get out of the way. Jesse pressed herself flat against the bitumen and covered her face with her hands. There was a mighty roar and a blast of hot air as the truck drove over her.

Fumes from hot oil and diesel fuel caught in her throat. She smothered a cough. Hard, gritty bitumen pressed against the back of her scalp.

As abruptly as it had approached, the truck passed. The air around her was fresh and open. Still she kept her hands glued to her face.

"Is she breathing ... did you get a licence number ... stop the traffic ... call an ambulance ..." A babble of voices floated above her. Fingers gently grasped her wrists and moved her hands away from her face.

"Are you all right?" asked a kindly female voice.

I can't see. For a second, Jesse panicked, then she realised that her eyes were still closed. She blinked rapidly. The sky seemed too bright.

A woman with wide green eyes and vivid red lipstick knelt beside her. "I'm a doctor. Are you hurting anywhere?"

"I don't think so." Jesse felt numb all over.

The doctor gently felt Jesse's head, arms and legs, then told her to take a few deep breaths. "No broken bones." The doctor held up a finger. "How many fingers do you see?"

"One."

"Now follow the movement." The doctor waved her hand from left to right. "Do you feel sick?"

In the background, drivers impatiently tooted car horns.

Jesse sat up. "No. I'm OK."

"Let's get you off the street." The woman doctor took hold of Jesse's right arm while a man in a striped suit took the left. Gently, they helped Jesse to her feet. "Move back, please."

Jesse looked around. "Where's Jasmine?"

No one answered. There was a ripple of movement, but none of the spectators retreated.

The doctor spoke again, this time more sharply, "Out of the way."

Jesse felt like a beetle mobbed by insane ants. She and her helpers shuffled towards the footpath. None of the faces peering at her were familiar.

A siren screamed louder and louder. An ambulance stopped.

Was Jasmine hurt? What if she'd hit her head or broken a bone? Jesse's heart pounded. Had the kidnappers staged the whole stunt, using the maroon car to separate them and snatch Jasmine?

Jesse screamed, "*Jasmine!*

16

"Jesse!"

Her knees wobbled at the sound of an answering cry.

Jasmine forced her way through the crowd.

A man and a woman in uniform, ambulance attendants, walked through the gap behind her. The woman carried a first aid box.

Jasmine slipped past them, dumped two backpacks at Jesse's feet and threw her arms around her in a fierce hug.

"You're all right!" said Jasmine.

"I would be if I could breathe."

Jasmine stepped back and grinned. Her palms were red where blood seeped through grazes.

The ambulance attendants took latex gloves from the first aid box. Jesse winced. The slapping of gloves reminded her of the C2 laboratory. The male attendant put out one hand. "You young ladies had better come with us."

Warning bells rang in Jesse's mind. "No!"

The two attendants frowned.

Jesse was determined. Jasmine was not going anywhere with two strangers. That long-haired man had been watching them, talking about them on his phone, and he knew Jesse's name. The maroon car had followed them, then almost run them down. How could she trust these ambulance attendants? They, too, could be part of a trap.

"I don't want to go to a hospital," said Jasmine. "I've only grazed my hands."

"Good thinking," said Jesse. "They jab you with needles, feed you mush and make you pee into pots."

Jasmine flinched. "I want to go home."

"We're fine. Look!" Jesse wriggled her arms and legs, flicking her head from left to right. *Ouch. Shouldn't have done that.*

A large man with a hairy chest peeking from a checked shirt stepped to the front. A frown brought his thick eyebrows dangerously close to his eyes. His hands were clenched. "I was driving that truck, Missie. What did you think you were doing?"

Does he think I rolled on to the road for fun? She could think of better ways to have fun. Rolling under trucks wouldn't even be in the top fifty.

"You could have been killed!" he said.

No kidding. Don't stand in a puddle – you'll get a brain wash. She was trying to be patient. He'd had a fright too. But being yelled at straight after being driven over by a truck was too much.

The man in the striped suit said, "I saw it happen. A maroon car came out of nowhere and ran the red light. This girl …" He pointed to Jesse, "leapt out of the way, but rolled straight into the path of your truck. The car's brakes must have failed."

A second siren began to wail. *Police? Uh oh.* Jesse wanted to avoid police officers. For starters, they would ask where she lived. And the questions would only get worse after that. Jesse could not give them answers.

With a grunt, the truck driver said, "Police will sort it out."

The female ambulance attendant stepped towards Jasmine. "Your hands need attention." She gestured towards the vehicle. "This way."

"We get sick in cars," said Jesse.

"Both of you?"

Jesse nodded. "We're really close."

The siren wailed louder.

Unnoticed, Jesse reached into her backpack and slipped a small object into her hand. She leant forward and whispered into Jasmine's ear, "Please do as I ask. Shut your eyes."

Jasmine obeyed.

She'd make a good spy. She runs fast and doesn't ask dumb questions.

Jesse aimed the object at the faces around her. Gasps erupted. People flung their hands over their eyes and cried out, "I can't see ... what happened ... it's a comet ..."

Actually it's an illuminator. It caused temporary flash blindness, like looking through dusty glass into bright sunlight.

The siren told Jesse that the police car was close. She grabbed Jasmine's arm, pulled her through the crowd and down a side alley. They turned left and right several times before Jesse felt safe.

"What happened back there?" asked Jasmine.

"Flashed a mirror," said Jesse. "They couldn't see for a minute."

She thought about what the man in the striped suit had said. He was wrong. The car driver had not braked. He had accelerated.

17

"Oowww."

"Keep still, Jasmine."

Jesse watched as Eva, the Carrillos" housekeeper, washed gravel and blood from Jasmine's hands.

"You should have seen Jesse. She moved like a rocket. I'd be minced on the road if it wasn't for her." Jasmine's voice was high-pitched and excited.

Eva raised an eyebrow at the word "minced'.

Perched on the huge black spa bath, Jesse looked at her reflection in the mirrored wall. A graze showed on her forehead. Her white T-shirt was filthy. *No big surprise.* It had been trodden on, rolled on bitumen and driven over. Her track pants had a hole over her right knee. She bent her right arm. It was tender. Bruises might show tomorrow. She put her special watch to her ear and shook it. No rattling. That was a good sign.

Gently, Eva taped a gauze bandage over each of

Jasmine's palms. "There. All fixed. Now I'll put on the kettle and make you two hot chocolate. And you'll both drink it."

Eva had an air of authority. She was tall and broad-shouldered, and her legs were almost too long to be real. *If Eva were a dog*, Jesse decided, *she'd be a great dane.*

"Are there any chocolate-chip biscuits?" asked Jasmine, a gleam in her eyes.

"Of course. Otherwise you'd gnaw the furniture." Eva winked at Jesse. Then she washed her hands and swished out the handbasin with fresh water. "Jasmine, I called your father. He should be home soon."

Jasmine screwed up her nose.

"I had to ring him for something like this. You know that." Eva left the bathroom.

"Jesse, you're a hero," said Jasmine.

"No, I'm not." Jesse felt her face go hot. "A hero wears tights and has a big *S* on his chest. I'm not doing tights for anyone."

"I can't believe you weren't squished by that truck." Jasmine shuddered.

"I'm thin. And I was in the middle of the chassis." Jesse shook her head to clear the mental image of a giant black wheel making her even thinner. She looked around the room. "Is this really your own bathroom?"

It was huge, with mirrored walls, hanging pot plants and a spa bath big enough to fit a whole basketball team.

"The rest of the house must be like a castle." Jesse was determined to see it all. She had a plan and she wasn't returning to C2 until she had completed it.

"My mum reckons she lost Dad in here for two days once. Couldn't find him. This house was Dad's idea. He has pots of money. He sends me to a state school because he doesn't want me to grow up soft."

Jesse didn't comment, but she thought plenty. *Is that a normal Dad thing to say or is Mr Carrillo strange?*

"Come on. I'll show you around." Jasmine beckoned Jesse to follow her back into the bedroom. It was elephant heaven. Her quilt cover had grey elephants marching across a yellow background. Wooden shelves held row after row of elephant statues and there was a giant poster of a mother and baby elephant. Jesse wished she could show Jasmine the special things in her own room, including the large blue footprints. But that was impossible.

"This is my family." Jasmine held up a photograph, careful to keep her bandaged palms away from the frame. "This is Dad." He had a square jaw, dark hair with grey flecks and smallish eyes. His stomach bulged over his belt.

"This is Mumll."

"Mumll?"

Jasmine nodded. "When I was little and learning to talk, I'd hear Dad say, *Mum'll do this* or *Mum'll do that*. So I started calling her *Mumll* and it's stuck."

Jasmine's mother had blonde hair curled up on top of her head, a longish nose and full lips. Her hands were folded gracefully on her lap. They looked as though they'd float into the air if Mrs Carrillo didn't hold them down.

"Mumll's in London for a few weeks. There's an Elvis display that she really wanted to see. You know what they've got in there? A vial of Elvis" sweat, a toenail and a wart on a pink cushion."

"A *wart*?"

"She's a fan." Jasmine said, as if that explained everything.

That was a long way and a lot of money to see a wart from a fat man with greasy hair.

"Miss Jasmine." A male voice drifted down the hallway.

"Yes?" Jasmine went to the open doorway.

"I heard what happened. Are you all right?"

Jesse listened carefully. *Is that voice familiar?*

Jasmine held up both her hands, palms out, to show the gauze bandages. "I'm OK. Thanks to my friend, Jesse."

A tall man with longish hair moved into the open doorway.

"Tom is head of security," said Jasmine. "He drinks lots of coffee and jangles keys."

The hairs on Jesse's arms stood to attention. She had seen Tom before. This morning he had sat beside a white van, spying on them.

18

'This hallway is the same size as a cricket pitch," said Jasmine.

"Do you ever play cricket in here?"

"No, but it feels cool saying that." Jasmine lowered her voice to a whisper. "Dad has this alarm system with these light beams across the hallway. Once Eva forgot and went downstairs to get her glasses and set them all off. Dad got such a fright he ran into a wall and gave himself a bloody nose."

Jesse filed the fact of the alarm system away in her mind.

"This is the dining room." Jasmine led her into another room on her right.

The walls were apricot. A large framed mirror hung on one wall and a painting of red flowers in a paddock on another. Dark polished wood sideboards lined the walls and there was a long table to match.

Running one hand along the shiny table, Jesse imagined the three Carrillos at one end, eating pasta. Or did they sit at opposite ends and shout? She touched the frame of the flower painting and quietly attached a metal listening device, the size of a lentil, to the back of it.

Jasmine spun round.

Jesse's heart thumped.

"Want to be posh and have our hot chocolate in here?" asked Jasmine.

"Great."

"You wait here and I'll go tell Eva, OK?"

Jesse nodded. It was more than OK. It was brilliant. She would have a few minutes alone.

She counted to twenty, then sneaked a look down the hallway. It was empty. Jesse crossed it and opened the opposite door. A sitting room, with a phone. *Excellent.* She pushed the door across without actually clicking it shut. Then she picked up the phone and tried to unscrew the mouthpiece. It was tight. She took a deep breath and tried again. *Whoever did this up was on steroids.*

She stopped, listening for footsteps. None. Although with this thick carpet, they would be hard to detect. "Make sure you get at least one into a phone," Liam had said.

Hot prickles on her skin made Jesse feel uncomfortable and sweaty.

One more twist and the end of the mouthpiece gave way. She fitted in the bugging device and screwed the top back down.

Abruptly the door swung open.

With the phone still in her hand, Jesse froze.

A stout man stood in the doorway. Jesse recognized him from the family photo. It was Jasmine's father, with a look on his face that would shrivel plants. "What are you doing in here?"

19

"I was ringing … home to say I was all right." Jesse put down the phone.

"Dad!" A hand snaked around the door and grabbed his sleeve.

He looked over his shoulder. "Jasmine."

She squeezed past him into the room. "This speeding car almost hit us. Jesse pushed me out of the way and a *truck* drove right over the top of her."

Mr Carrillo focused on the graze on Jesse's forehead. His face hardened. Jesse guessed that he was angry at the careless driver. Except that the driver hadn't been careless. He had driven straight at them. Who was he? C2 or an enemy of the Carrillo family?

"Are you both OK?"

Both girls talked over the top of each other to reassure him.

Mr Carrillo advanced towards Jesse. Not sure what

he intended, she was ready to run. But he smiled and held out his right hand.

She shook it.

"Thank you for looking out for my daughter."

"Yoo hoo. Where is everyone?" Eva's voice, along with the chink of mugs, drifted into the room from the hallway.

Jesse's spirits lifted at the thought of chocolate-chip biscuits.

Back in the dining room, Mr Carrillo sat and watched the two girls drink hot chocolate and demolish biscuits. He tried to make conversation. Jesse wished he wouldn't. He ran through a list of questions, ordinary for most people, but dangerous for her. *Where do you live, what do your parents do, how long have you known Jasmine, where were you before this*?

Was he like this with all of Jasmine's friends?

Jesse sipped her chocolate. It was thick and sweet. "What is your job, Mr Carrillo?"

"Trade." Absent-mindedly, he rubbed at the back of his neck.

When is an answer not an answer? When Mr Carrillo speaks but doesn't tell me anything. "What do you trade?"

"Goods."

She wanted to ask more, but it would seem too nosy.

"Jasmine. Question for the week," he said.

Laughing, she explained to Jesse. "Every week Dad gives me a question and I have to find the answer."

"Are the North Pole and the South Pole the same temperature?"

Automatically, Jesse shook her head.

"Jesse," he said. "You know the answer?"

"Elevation. One is higher than the other and ..." Suddenly Jesse realised that Jasmine and her father were staring at her. She swallowed the rest of the answer. Most people wouldn't know facts like that. Jesse shrugged. "At my last school I had a project about it. That's all I remember."

Curiosity satisfied, Jasmine concentrated on her chocolate.

Mr Carrillo stood up. "Well, now that I know you're all right, I'll head back to work."

Nodding, Jasmine bit into a biscuit.

"And thank you, Jesse. I'm glad my daughter has such a good friend."

Jesse smiled. *What would he think if he knew who I really am?*

He walked towards the door, stopped beside a cupboard and opened the top drawer. Unexpectedly, he spun round. "Catch!"

Jesse felt, rather than saw, a small blur shoot through

the air towards her. Instinctively, she threw up one hand and batted the object back. *A tennis ball?* Mr Carrillo tried to catch it in return, but he was too slow. The ball bounced off his forearm on to the floor, then rolled under the table.

"Good reflexes," he said.

"Dad!" Jasmine's aggrieved voice rang out.

Jesse stared at Mr Carrillo's shirt sleeve. Blood seeped through the blue material. He covered the patch with one hand. "It's nothing. I cut myself at work. I should have put a bandaid over it. The ball just hit the spot. My own fault." He glanced sideways as he spoke.

Is he embarrassed? thought Jesse.

"Dad's always goofing round. He thinks he's funny. You see why Mumll wanted to get away and look at a wart?" Jasmine giggled. A second Carrillo who thought she was funny. But this time Jesse agreed.

Jesse sighed. Her first visit to Jasmine's house, and already she'd narrowly missed being caught planting a bug in the phone and made Mr Carrillo's arm bleed. Although Mr Carrillo didn't have to throw the ball that hard. It was a full-on pitch, aimed straight at her face. What if she'd missed?

"You've got a mark on your head." Liam's hands, which held the steering wheel, were grubby, the nails stained brown around the edges.

"Got to expect that when you're run over by a truck." Jesse kicked a cardboard container aside and stretched out her feet. After today, Liam's clunky little car seemed familiar, safe.

"Nasty. How's the truck?"

Jesse glanced sideways, but Liam's face was impassive.

"What happened?" he asked.

As he drove back to C2, she told him.

"Did you get into the main rooms?" he asked.

"Yes. But I was almost caught by Mr Carrillo putting a bug in the phone."

"Almost is OK. Means he missed. You'll get better at it."

Better? Jesse hoped she'd never have to do that again.

It still made her shiver to think of that moment.

"I saw you go in the house with the girl," said Liam.

"Her name's Jasmine."

Liam grunted.

"I didn't see *you*," said Jesse.

"You weren't supposed to."

"That security man, Tom, who spied on us at school, knew my name. Is he from C2?"

"No. But part of his job is to keep an eye on the girl..."

"Jasmine."

He braked to avoid a puppy with long ears, who scampered willy-nilly across the street. "Don't get personally involved. It'll only cause you heartache and you won't do your job properly. We complete our assignment. We go home. The next shift goes to work. Then we move on to the next job."

"Ever thought about changing jobs?"

"You don't leave C2."

Want to bet?

Liam turned the car right. Soon they would be at the C2 car park.

"But if this Tom was watching Jasmine, that means he knows about the kidnap threat," said Jesse. "I thought the family didn't know."

"Maybe he was watching her for other reasons."

What reasons? To Jesse, it seemed bizarre that a family

would assign someone to watch their kid at school. *But what do I know about families?*

"So if Tom is just security..."

"Nobody is *just* anything. Not even us. The friendliest face can hide the most treacherous thoughts. Don't trust him."

"But you just said..."

"Don't trust *me*."

"I..."

"Don't trust yourself."

21

"What did you think of Carrillo?" asked Liam.

Jesse shrugged. "He's a bit strange."

"How?"

Immediately, she thought of the tennis ball. "His jokes aren't funny."

"Most jokes aren't. People laugh because they want to please the person who told the joke."

"I think he could have a temper. He cares about Jasmine. He's intelligent."

The lights changed. Liam accelerated. "Carrillo has some shady business partners. I wonder if this kidnap threat is something to do with that. It's all so vague. I've learnt that he's arranging a shipment this weekend. I'd like to know what's in it. His background check shows no arrests. Just a few speeding tickets. He gained distinctions in university. Lived in Switzerland for several years. Has a beautiful wife, an adoring child, a mansion. It's all too perfect. Too clean. Most people's lives are a mess. Not his. What's been covered up?"

Jesse was confused. How could someone look suspicious because they *hadn't* done anything? "The kidnap threat might be about money."

"Possibly. But thugs don't usually ask for the ransom *before* they kidnap the victim."

"So we don't know who made the threat?"

Liam shook his head. "It was a tip-off. Granger wouldn't give away his source. Must be someone under deep cover. But if C2 is involved, then this Carrillo is important to them. He must be providing a service or product they don't want to lose."

"Or he knows something about them that's secret."

"In that case, he might just disappear."

A chill ran through Jesse as she thought of Rohan.

"The kidnap threat could be to manipulate him, to make him do something … or *not* do something. The child is his soft spot, perhaps – his weakness."

If so, Jesse could understand why. Jasmine was great. Even if there was no assignment, Jesse would like to be her friend. *Does that make Jasmine my weakness too?*

22

Jesse had her smile ready as the office waiting room door opened. In her mind, she had practised this moment, but actually saying the words was harder. She had never asked Prov for anything really big. CDs and videos, sure. The ones Mary supplied were boring. But this was different.

Prov wore another short-sleeved mohair top. This time it was pink. *Did she have a rule – any colour, but must have lots of fluff?*

"Here's my daily report for Director Granger." Jesse placed a large envelope on the desk. Inside were several sheets of paper and a computer disk.

Prov punched a list of numbers into the small safe beside her desk and slipped it inside. "He's out. I'll give it to him when he returns ... what's that mark on your forehead?"

"Stupid door. I should have looked where I was

going." Jesse wondered if other field agents blamed doors for their injuries. Maybe she should have come up with something more creative.

Prov gave her a penetrating look, but asked no more questions.

Jesse leant forward and whispered. "Is this room bugged?" Her breath did not disturb Prov's hair one bit. She used so much spray, Jesse doubted a hurricane would ruffle it.

Prov whispered back, "I presume you don't mean cockroaches?"

Jesse cupped one hand to her ear to mime "listening'.

Prov shook her head, but kept her voice quiet. "Director Granger is strict about that. He's fanatical about security. At the end of every day we back up files, twice, and someone sweeps these rooms for listening devices. The walls and doors are especially thick and constructed of special materials, so longer range devices won't penetrate."

"What if the person sweeping for bugs actually planted one?"

"I doubt it." Prov frowned. "No, I'm *sure* of it. It's always a different agent who does it. They'd all have to be in on it to keep a bug here." Sympathy softened her face. "What's wrong?"

"Who am I?" Jesse knelt beside her. "Mary won't tell

me. I don't know who my parents were or how the car accident happened. Have I other relatives? How did C2 find me? I was only one year old. How did they know I was a prodigy?"

Prov touched Jesse's hair with one hand. "I can't answer those questions. I don't know. When I came here, you'd already been here two years and that woman was looking after you."

To Prov, it was always "that woman" and not Mary.

Jesse peeked at the computer screen. "There must be records. The scientists, Roger and Michael, have done tests in the laboratory. They write things down. If I've been legally adopted, there'll be information about it."

Prov flushed as though someone had turned up the heating. "I can't access many of the files. If they're marked *Top secret* or *Director's eyes only* then I'm shut out."

Jesse had hacked into other computer systems outside C2. However, they were simple compared to this one. There were electronic safeguards that she couldn't break through.

"There must be other ways to get some information."

"Some of the older material is on paper, down in the basement. Not on computer." Prov chewed on her bottom lip. "I only have access to basic material."

"You have security clearance and you're the only one I trust," said Jesse. "What happens to the back-up disks?"

"I shouldn't tell you this … but if I were you, I'd want to know about my family. And it's time someone looked after you better." Prov looked over at the closed door. "One set of disks is locked in a safe in the Director's office and the others go to the archives. The archives have more security devices than his office. Sensitive files and disks have a tag attached which gives out a radio signal. If one is removed, security would know in a second."

"Oh."

"You'd better go. Granger will be back any minute. But a good office manager might make another copy of special files, just for safe keeping … I can't promise … I'd have to be careful. So would you."

"I don't want you to lose your job."

Prov's pupils grew so big they became black holes. "Honey, it's not my job that I'm worried about."

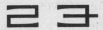

The hands on the back-to-front clock showed Jai was late. Jesse spun on her chair to face the door. Was he sick?

He has one more minute then I'm going to find him.

Just then, soft footsteps announced Jai's arrival. His shoulders were slumped and his arms dangled loosely at his sides as though he didn't know what to do with them.

"Where's your violin?" asked Jesse.

"Michael took it away. He wants to see how it will affect me to be without my music."

Not well, judging by the dark shadows under Jai's eyes.

It still surprised Jesse that freaky men in white coats, who spent their lives doing experiments on children and inventing bizarre weapons, would have ordinary names like Michael or Roger.

"They didn't hurt you, did they?" Jesse locked the door.

He shook his head.

"Why don't you sit down? We can talk tonight. No games."

He didn't argue, just flopped on to the orange sofa, ignoring the giant blue footsteps.

"I can play my clarinet for you if you like." Jesse had only learnt it so that the scientists could gauge her aptitude for music. She proved she could play. Now she didn't need to do it.

"I am not that distressed," he said with a slight smile.

Jesse understood completely.

"I was in the laboratory all day."

"Want a drink?" Jesse opened the small fridge in the corner of her room, took out a jug of fresh orange juice and two glasses. She took one glass across to Jai and kept the other for herself.

He drained the juice in the same time that Jesse had taken two sips.

"Do you have anything to eat?" His eyes showed that his stomach was more demanding than his polite voice.

Jesse pulled out a couple of apples, an orange, a boiled egg and a slice with red dots. "Mary's into lentils this week." Jesse dropped the slice into the rubbish bin.

Jai crunched the apple like a piranha attacking a carcass. The colour returned to his cheeks, although the smudges beneath his eyes stayed.

"What happened to your head?" *Crunch*, another lump of apple disappeared into Jai's mouth.

"Um …"

Munch. He shook his head. "Forget that I asked."

Fair enough. She couldn't tell him the truth anyway.

"You have a question to ask me?"

She started with surprise. "How do you know?"

Crunch. "It is in your eyes even if it is not yet on your lips. Your movements are faster than usual. You are slightly agitated." He put a finger to his lips and raised his eyebrows.

"I've already scanned for bugs. The room is clean."

"What is your question?"

"Has anyone told you about where you come from? Which country? Who your parents were, anything like that?"

"No. Jesse, we have had this conversation before."

"I know. But I want to be sure. Why haven't they told us anything?"

"They may think it would unsettle us. Perhaps we are more docile if we know nothing."

"Don't you think it's strange?" she asked.

"This place is all I have ever known. Sometimes it is hard to know if things are strange or perfectly normal."

"The man I'm working with told me there are more child prodigies in C2. In other branches."

Jai blinked several times. "Who are they? How many are there?"

"I don't know. He only told me about one boy. Interstate. But the way he said it … I think there are even more."

"Did you ask him about it?"

"I couldn't," said Jesse. "I don't think he likes me. And he hates questions. Even if I asked him, he'd probably just lie."

"He might have been lying when he told you there were more of us."

"I don't think so. And if I ask too many questions, they'll know I'm interested. They might bury the truth even deeper. We'd never find out anything."

Jai nodded. "Agreed."

"How can we all be orphans? And I want to show you something." She sat on her computer chair, gave her fingerprints, then her four passwords and logged on to the Internet. "I entered the words *missing children* into a search engine."

Jai ditched his apple core into the bin. It looked like a tiny animal spine without flesh.

"This is about *Operation Babylift*. In 1975, after the war, nearly 3,000 orphans were taken from orphanages and child care centres in Vietnam. Some of those children had parents. They were stolen. There was a big court case about it," she explained.

"We are too young to be connected to that. And you are obviously not Vietnamese."

"No." Jesse turned her head to look at him. "But you could be. Jai, if one government ordered their agents to do that, why not others? And if they've stolen children once, they might do it again. It wouldn't have to be in Vietnam. There's always a war somewhere. Kids go missing."

He stared at the computer screen.

Jesse thought of C2's laboratory. "This says they used these kids for experiments."

"You cannot believe everything you read on the Internet," he said, yet there was curiosity in his tone.

"Jai, what if we're not really orphans, but were stolen from our families?'

24

Jesse's stomach rumbled as she peered through Liam's car window at a hamburger shop. Today, she hadn't fallen under a truck, balanced on a toilet seat to eavesdrop, or injured her only friend's father. *I might be getting the hang of this spy stuff.* Part of her felt she shouldn't be going back to C2 yet. Not enough had happened. Yet spending another day with Jasmine had been a treat.

"What do you think of school?" Liam asked.

"Boring."

"Ha. This was only your second day. You should try a second year or a second decade. I was always in trouble in school. Had a learning disability. The dopey kid who didn't know what was going on. So I played up, to hide it."

Did he have smelly sneakers like Hugh? Bet he did. "You're not dopey now."

"No."

"You're cranky though."

"Yeah. But only when I'm on assignment with an agent who sucks her thumb."

They both faced the front of the car, satisfied with the score – one hit each.

As they neared C2, Jesse felt herself tense, as though invisible ropes tightened around her chest.

Liam drove down to the level below the basement and stopped. He scooped up paper from the floor of his car and began shoving it into a cardboard container.

Jesse grabbed her bag, got out and leant against the car. Liam had enough paper in there to make a whole tree. Suddenly she became aware of something out of place. Without moving her body, she scanned the car park. What was it?

Liam was still in the car, head down, rummaging in rubbish. If she called out to him, it would attract attention. Better to keep still and listen. *There. It's scraping. Faint, but definite.* Jesse deliberately yawned. "Rats, my shoelace is undone again." Casually, she placed her bag on the bonnet and knelt down. Fiddling with her laces, she looked left and right beneath the cars. *No feet showing.* She checked left a second time. Damp footprints led from a puddle to a parked car, then stopped. Yet no driver was visible.

Here we go again. Jesse wondered if every field assignment included crawling around in car parks. She hoped not. Hands on the concrete, she scuttled wide around the suspicious area. Warily, she raised her head, gasped, then ducked down again.

A man crouched in the open doorway of a green car, knees bent, his feet still on the car floor. He balanced himself with his left hand. *That's why I didn't see his feet.* In his right hand he held a gun. It was aimed directly at Liam. In a moment the man would wonder why it took Jesse so long to retie her shoelace and become suspicious. She had to act now.

Still hunkered down, she slipped around another car and came up behind the man. Hard and swift, she punched him exactly six centimetres below his right shoulder.

"What..." The gun fell on to the concrete.

Before he could respond, Jesse karate chopped him on the side of his neck. He crumpled backwards in an untidy heap, still with a surprised expression on his face.

Liam bent over the unconscious man's body. "What did you do?"

"I applied pressure to his brachial plexus tie-in, then chopped the brachial plexus origin," said Jesse.

"You did *what*?" He scratched his head.

"I paralyzed his arm so he'd drop the gun, then applied a karate chop to the base of his neck. An artery and several nerves run through that area. If you hit it, you disrupt the blood flow and the person falls unconscious."

"Thanks for the lesson, Master Karate girl. I thought you did tae kwon do."

"I have a black belt in that. I've dabbled in karate. I didn't find it as interesting."

Liam picked up the man's gun, checked it, then slid it back into the man's pocket.

"You're giving him back his gun!"

"That's right."

"But he was going to shoot you."

"Jesse, meet Hans Faulkner. He's an agent with C2. You've just knocked out one of our own men."

Jesse gasped. "What'll we do?"

"Get out of here before he wakes up."

"But we can't just leave him here. He might be hurt."

Liam rolled his eyes, then knelt beside Agent Faulkner. He pressed two fingers gently under his jaw. "Strong pulse. He's fine." Liam stood and began to walk away. "Come on."

Reluctantly, Jesse followed.

"You're a funny one," he said. "You don't think twice about knocking people out, then you go weak at the knees in case they're hurt."

"Why was he trying to shoot you?"

Back at the car, Liam grabbed Jesse's bag and thrust it into her arms. "Here, partner. Carry your own gear. This isn't a charity. Hans wasn't going to shoot. Sneaky sod. I didn't know he was back. Caught me by surprise. We have this challenge between us, to catch the other unawares. Keeps us on our toes."

"I thought I was putting my life in danger to save you and it was only a game?" She glared at him. "I could have died from fright."

"I owe you one."

Jesse stared at Liam's neck and imagined the exact spot she would like to chop.

Jesse stomped along the corridor towards her room.

"Jesse!"

She looked up to see Prov. Had she found something in the files? Jesse's eyes flicked towards the security cameras fixed to the ceilings. They would be following everything that happened out here. But Prov knew that.

She held something in her hands. "Honey, I made you this no-bake cheesecake."

Now she was close, Jesse could smell the strong sweetness of Prov's perfume. A speck of eyeliner sat like a freckle on her eyelid. A pulse beat rapidly in her neck.

She's nervous.

Prov leant forward to plant a peck on Jesse's cheek and whispered, "There's a special ingredient."

Jesse wondered if she had red lipstick on her cheek now, but she didn't mind. She took the cheesecake and sniffed it. "Thank you. It smells wonderful. Just like lemons."

"Hold it right there," came a tight voice from behind.

Prov and Jesse spun round.

Mary Holt stood like a soldier guarding a treasure. "What is that?"

"A cheesecake." Jesse held it closer to her body.

"Give it to me." Mary held out both hands. "You are not permitted such appallingly rubbishy food. Healthy body, healthy mind."

She'd said that so often, in the same sing-song tone, that Jesse wondered if her voice was actually a recording. If the food police were after new recruits, Mary should be number one on their list.

"It's not for me personally, Mary." Jesse used her sweetest voice. "It's for … well, I can't say where I'm going each day. But I need this for tomorrow."

A frown wrinkled Mary's brow. "Why would you need a cake for a field assignment?"

"Top secret. Prov doesn't know what I want it for either…"

"No, I know nothing." Prov's voice was too loud and shrill.

Mary pouted. "I don't believe that a cheesecake could be top secret."

Why not? Everything else is around here.

"I wouldn't either, if I were you," said Jesse.

Prov gasped.

"Sounds silly. But it's true. Why don't you check with Director Granger, if you're worried?"

If Mary called her bluff and went to Granger, she was sunk. Jesse watched the expressions on Mary's face change as she imagined herself confronting the Director of C2 to ask if Jesse could take a cheesecake on her secret assignment. She also saw the moment Mary decided to stop arguing.

"Why didn't you ask me? I'm your carer."

"I know you prefer healthy food. I thought you might feel bad making something like this."

Mary's face settled into its normal discontented lines. "Yes, well. I do my duty. But you ... Provincial, or whatever your real name is ... you're not supposed to be on this level. Off you go." She made shooing noises as though she were rounding up chickens.

Prov didn't argue. She patted Jesse on the back and retreated.

Slow down, Prov, Jesse told her silently. *You look like you're running away.*

Mary sniffed. "I hope you will be responsible and not nibble any of that. It will rot your teeth. And too much sugar gives you a false energy high, then you crash and feel more tired."

"Yes, Mary."

"You'd better put it in the fridge straight away." She

looked at her watch. "You're late. They want you in the laboratory."

Jesse felt a sick taste at the back of her throat.

⊒ ⁊

"Ten more, Jesse. You can do it."

Puffing, her arms beginning to wobble, Jesse tried another push-up. "Thirty-one, thirty-two…" She was sick of seeing carpet pile under her nose.

Michael stood beside her with a clipboard, watching. Sometimes Jesse felt like doing something totally outrageous, to see his reaction.

"Thirty-nine, forty." She flopped on the carpet, sweat running down her temples. That was it. She'd been exercising for an hour. At least this session hadn't included anything weird or too uncomfortable. Her regular exercise routine was bearable.

Michael scribbled on his clipboard.

You'd think he'd be more into computers than clipboards.

"Wrist."

Jesse held out her wrist. Michael felt for her pulse,

checking it against his watch. Then he wrote on the clipboard again. "You know what's next."

Grudgingly, Jesse scrambled to her feet. "Do I have to?"

He nodded.

"But I hate needles."

"A vitamin B12 supplement is good for you."

"Someone who has a perfectly balanced diet, as I do, does not need vitamin supplements."

He rubbed a small spot on her arm with disinfectant on gauze, then inserted the needle.

Ouch, thought Jesse, but she refused to flinch.

"We've missed you, Jesse."

Yeah right.

Two good things came from her field assignment. Making a friend and being away from C2.

Someone appeared in the gymnasium doorway.

Jesse turned.

"Good afternoon," said Director Granger, "Glad to see you're keeping fit."

As if I had a choice.

"Michael. Would you leave us for a few minutes?"

Michael retreated to the back room and closed the door.

If only it were that easy for me. Michael, would you go away? Great. Michael, stick that needle in your own arm. Excellent. Michael, a hundred push-ups, now.

Michael, lock yourself in that tub of water with no light or sound and see how long before you crack. Fantastic.

The Director slipped his hands into his pockets. "Liam tells me you have asked permission to stay at the target's house tomorrow night."

Jesse felt hope sink like a heavy weight at the coldness in his voice. "Yes, I can be closer to her there, watch what goes on at the house." Jesse wiped sweat from her brow with her right forearm. She wanted to stay at Jasmine's so much it hurt. But if Director Granger knew that, he might say no.

He pursed his lips.

If the answer's no, then just tell me.

"It's a good opportunity to observe the household at close range," he said. "And Liam says you can be trusted."

"He *did*?" Maybe this is what he meant in the car park by *I owe you one*.

Granger raised one eyebrow. "You sound surprised."

"I thought he didn't like me."

"He doesn't have to. He just has to do his job. That's all. Every action has consequences. Liam would not enjoy the consequences of failure. Neither would you."

The door was locked, the room free from listening devices and there was half an hour till lights out. Jesse slid her fingers under the cheesecake, hoping she was right about Prov's "special ingredient'.

The crumbed base was rough on her fingers. *Nothing hidden there.* She looked at the soft, yellow mixture in the middle. It was going to make a big mess, but there was no other way. *One ... two ... three.* She plunged her hand into the middle, not sure whether to say "yuck" because it was gooey or "yum" because it was probably delicious.

No wonder Prov worked in the office and not on field assignments. There must be better ways to hide something than in the middle of a cake. But then, how many people would think of searching a cheesecake for secret material?

Ah, there it is. Jesse pulled out a computer disk

protected by a zip-lock bag. She placed it carefully on a tissue beside her computer. The disk itself was perfectly clean.

She looked at the ruined cheesecake with regret. If Mary saw it like this, she might guess the truth. Reluctantly, Jesse picked up the plate, held it at shoulder height and turned it upside down. It splattered onto the floor, splashing onto Jesse's trousers.

"Oops. Sorry, Mary. I had an accident," she said under her breath, then licked her fingers. Yes, that was a definite *yum*.

She washed her hands at double speed, eager to get to her computer.

It was only seconds before the machine was fired up and ready to go, but it seemed longer. With trembling fingers, Jesse inserted the disk. Her hand hovered over the mouse. What if she discovered something she would rather not know?

29

The file began with facts about Jesse's weight and height at different ages. And a series of photographs. She didn't have a camera, had no photos of her own. Michael and Roger had conducted hundreds of tests and refused to tell her the results or why they did them. So when they took the annual photographs she never asked to see them.

Looking at this toddler, then the bigger child, was like staring at a stranger. *Is that really me?* Through different hairstyles and facial expressions one thing remained the same – a determined glint in the eyes.

If only there was a photo of the three of them, Rohan, Jai and herself, together.

She checked the time. *Twenty minutes till lights out. Better hurry up. I can look at these again later.*

A quick scroll down brought her to "Personality Profile at Four Years of Age."

Jesse Sharpe has an extraordinary memory.

She is a natural mimic.

The child shows signs of stubbornness, a trait that could lead her either to become a determined, hardworking adult or to develop an inability to compromise.

She interacts well with the other children and acts protectively towards them. She seems distrustful of adults. She may be a cautious adult, or she may become cynical.

Her language skills are outstanding. She reads a wide range of books and has mastered Spanish, English and French.

She shows an advanced interest in mathematics and physics.

This child does not like to be given orders. She responds better to suggestions.

Currently, there is no sign of mental instability.

We feel that Jesse Sharpe has proved a good candidate for Operation IQ. However, she will need discipline and close supervision to ensure that her individuality does not affect her usefulness.

Recommended to continue with the program.

Jesse sat back in her chair. *Recommended to continue*

with the program – what if their conclusion had been different? What would have happened to her?

And why would they look for signs of "mental instability'? Were they expecting some?

She clicked on a scanned newspaper article. The headline said, "Child Found in Car with Dead Parents'. A man and woman had been driving in their car. Another vehicle, speeding, had not given way and rammed into this couple's car. The car rolled and the couple were killed. A baby girl was found alive, but unconscious, strapped into a car seat.

Jesse felt the strength drain out of her. Her legs were heavy and useless. It must be true. She really *was* an orphan. Until now, her parents had been shadows. If she turned, they weren't there, had *never* been there. But now she had a sense that they had been real people. Sadness swept through her. She felt as though she had glimpsed them, for a brief second, then they vanished again.

There was no copy of adoption papers.

Near the bottom of the file it read, "Further information classified TOP SECRET. RESTRICTED ACCESS. OPERATION IQ'.

Jesse tapped the screen. *That's where the real information is kept and I can't touch it. Not yet.*

Then she read, "CROSS REFERENCE OPERATION IQ" and it listed four different states. Were all the C2 child prodigies orphans? That was impossible. Maybe their parents had volunteered them for the project. But why?

But Jesse, Rohan and Jai had been told that they were orphans and had no one to look after them. C2 had stepped in to save them – so they said.

Jesse took out the disk and prepared to hide it in her secret place. She told no one where it was. Not even Jai. If anyone found the disk, Prov would be in danger. And no matter how much Jesse wanted to find out about her past, she couldn't let that happen.

The information on the disk was a beginning. There was a lot more. Jesse resolved to find out everything. Not today. Not tomorrow. But she *would* find out.

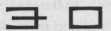

Jesse tugged the blanket up to her chin. She wasn't cold, just relished being wrapped in a soft blanket. Jesse was still shocked that Director Granger had given permission for her to stay overnight at Jasmine's house. *But here I am.*

It was Jasmine's turn to ask two questions. "Favourite colour?"

"Yellow."

"Favourite food?"

"Um ... hamburger." *Because I've never tasted one,* Jesse added silently.

Jasmine laughed. "Your go."

Jesse stretched, touching the end of the trundle bed with her toes. "Best TV show?"

"Documentaries on elephants."

"Scariest person you've ever met?" Jesse wondered if Jasmine's answer would give her a clue about who was threatening her.

"Me. Because I have to take myself everywhere I go. So if I don't like myself, I'm stuck with me."

Cool answer, but no help as a clue.

In the pale glow from the ensuite nightlight, Jesse saw Jasmine turn over. "I'm glad you came to our school."

"So am I," said Jesse. "Do you get scared in this big house at night?"

"No. Security patrols outside. And inside, there's the alarm system upstairs and downstairs. When Dad's out, like tonight, Eva or Mumll are usually home. Besides, who'd want to break in here?"

Good question. Jesse felt comforted that her own security patrol of one – Liam – was also outside.

Jasmine's voice softened, became furry. "I'm nearly asleep."

"Me too. Good night." Jesse waited till Jasmine snuffled in a way that suggested she was truly asleep.

Adrenalin kicked in, making Jesse's heart race. Carefully, she eased back the blanket and stood up.

Jasmine didn't move.

First Jesse slipped on a pair of goggles, then a pair of latex gloves. Her stomach turned at the feel of the gloves, but she didn't want her fingerprints to turn up in the wrong places. She hoisted her shoulder bag, then crept to the door and peeked out. Through the goggles, she saw beams of infra-red light criss-crossing the hallway. If she touched any of them, an alarm would sound.

The first beam was about a metre above the floor. Jesse flattened herself on the carpet and wriggled like a worm. The carpet smelt dusty but she didn't dare lift her head. Clutching her shoulder bag firmly to her side, she stepped over the second beam. Gradually she worked her way safely along the hallway.

She listened for sounds. Nothing. She turned the handle of Mr Carrillo's office. Locked, as she'd suspected. She took a thin metal tool from her shoulder bag, hoping the door itself wasn't alarmed. How would she explain standing in the hall, wearing this wild gear and fiddling with the lock?

Quietly, she pushed the tool into the lock, easing it left then right. Sensing the moment it clicked, rather than hearing it, she turned the door handle a second time. This time it swung open. Jesse sighed with relief. No alarm.

Stepping inside, she closed the door gently behind her. She took off the goggles, placed them in the shoulder bag and took out a small torch. *Ah, there's the computer, in the corner near the window.*

Once the screen lit up, she didn't need the torch and switched it off.

OK, what would Mr Carrillo's password be? People usually chose predictable, easily remembered passwords, their birth dates or names of family members. What about his wife's name, *Julianna?* "Incorrect password." His daughter, *Jasmine?* "Incorrect password." Jesse swung on the chair. *Ah, I know.* She typed in *MumII.* The computer whirred. She was in. Only one password. That was slack, and dangerous. People could break in.

She went straight for his emails. Mr Carrillo had deleted his messages. *So he thinks.* Silently, Jesse thanked Rohan for all the computer tricks he had shown her. She used to tease him by saying he had an electronic mouse instead of a dummy when he was a baby.

As always, the thought of Rohan made her sad. She shook her head. *I must concentrate.*

Nothing on computers was truly deleted. It was electronically chopped up and scattered. She searched among the debris on the hard drive. The scraps she found were mostly boring – business meeting arrangements, a birthday greeting, chatty nonsense. Then she found a large part of a message to his wife. There was no word about Jasmine's tangle with the maroon car. It did say Jasmine had a new friend, so it must have been sent recently. Maybe he didn't want to worry his wife while she was away.

What's this? She found part of a sent message that

made her eyes grow wide. *This must be a mistake.* She re-read the message, twice. It wasn't all retrievable, but it was enough to make her sweat. She couldn't think of another way to interpret the information. Mr Carrillo had arranged to have his own daughter kidnapped.

ᴲ1

Is Mr Carrillo crazy?

If he didn't like his daughter or wanted her out of the way, why didn't he send her overseas with her mother or put her in a boarding school? He didn't have to kidnap her. Unless he wanted her hidden from someone else who threatened her. They couldn't take her if she had already disappeared. *This is so weird and so complicated.*

Just a minute. Jesse's brain spun like a satellite out of control. *C2 are smart enough to have bugs planted inside the house and agents watching the Carrillos. Liam says they're using scanners to eavesdrop on his mobile phone conversations. How could they overlook emails?*

Suddenly suspicious, she checked further for hidden software designed to pick up emails. Mr Carrillo might not think to look for something like that.

There it is. C2 must know about that email. Why

haven't they taken Carrillo away? And if they think he's going to fake a kidnapping, to remove Jasmine from the real danger, why haven't they told me?

Until she knew what was going on, she had to get Jasmine out of here. But where could they go? If C2 were involved, Jesse couldn't take her there. *One step at a time. When we're away from here, we'll figure out what to do.*

What do I say to Jasmine? Excuse me, but we have to run away, right now, because your father plans to kidnap you. Jesse could hardly believe it herself, but somehow, she had to convince Jasmine.

Shaking slightly, she closed down the computer and refitted the goggles. She opened the door and looked out. Every nerve in her body jumped to attention. No beams of infra-red light criss-crossed the long hallway. The alarm was off. Had Carrillo's security team discovered her presence in the office? Or did this mean something worse?

She ripped off the goggles and gloves, stuffed them into the bag and shot down the hallway. One hand on the doorframe, Jesse swung into Jasmine's room.

A soft glow from the nightlight showed crumpled blankets and a pillow half-hanging off the mattress. Jasmine's bed was empty.

The door swung open and caught her on the arm.

She staggered sideways. Rough, heavy material was thrown over her head. Strong arms wrapped around her tightly. Jesse struggled. The material pressed against her face, making it hard to breathe. Her knees buckled.

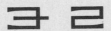

Jesse felt consciousness return slowly. She opened her eyes but her vision was still cloudy. A few blinks and a deep breath later, the room cleared. She lay on her side on a couch, her wrists and ankles tied together. Wide tape covered her mouth.

I'm still alive. That's a good sign, isn't it? But wait till they find out they've kidnapped the wrong girl. They'll be furious. Or did they take me because I blundered in before they could escape? In that case, they have Jasmine captive too. Jesse's stomach turned. *Please be all right, Jasmine.*

Answers to those questions would have to wait. Her priority was to get out. She lifted her head. The room was neat, clean, and had no windows. There was a sink, the couch on which she lay, a rickety cupboard against one wall and not much else. The concrete floor was swept clean.

Jesse tugged at the bindings on her hands. There was some slack there. Whoever had tied her up had left a short strand of tape between each wrist. She could move a little and it didn't interfere with her circulation. A kind captor – or one who hadn't had much practice? Still, the ties wouldn't break. Fiercely, she tried to snap the duct tape by forcing her wrists apart. Until they began to ache with the effort and the tape ripped at the tiny hairs on her arms.

Maybe it would be easier to nibble through the mouth tape first. She rested a moment, then tried to open her lips. Little by little, she pinched the tape between her front teeth. It was tough stuff. She felt like a giant rabbit gnawing at bark.

A key turned in the lock. Someone was coming in. She closed her eyes, forcing herself to relax, as though she were still unconscious. *Breathe slowly. Don't let your eyelids flicker.*

The door opened with a squeak. Footsteps approached. Jesse longed to peek, but she didn't dare. A second set of feet, probably belonging to a heavier person, stepped inside the room and stopped. Cool fingers felt under her neck for a pulse, then pressed gently against her forehead.

"Pulse is fine, no temperature. Her colour's good. She should come round any time." The voice was female and

Jesse recognised it. *Eva, the Carrillos" housekeeper.*

"Lucky for you," added Eva. "Did you have to be so rough? You could have suffocated her."

"What was I supposed to do – let her kick her way free and run straight to C2?" said an unfamiliar male voice.

C2? They know where I'm from.

Eva spoke again. "I'll check her again in half an hour. By then she'll need the bathroom and something to eat. The procedure will have to wait till tomorrow."

What procedure? Jesse felt sick.

The two sets of footsteps retreated and the door was locked again.

Jesse opened her eyes. A terrifying thought ripped through her mind. The target hadn't been Jasmine Carrillo – it was Jesse Sharpe.

She had half an hour to figure out a plan. First she had to break free of this tape. She couldn't open her mouth wide. *There must be another way.* Her hands were useless at her back. *If I can get them to the front, it'd be much better.*

Squeezing her knees up into her chest, she rolled herself into a tight ball. Then she forced her hands down, trying to ease them around her body. Her arms screamed at her to stop, to release the pressure. *You can't dislocate a joint doing this, can you?*

Come on, you can do it. One more try. She let out her breath and curled up a fraction tighter. *If only my arms were longer.* Suddenly, they slipped around her body.

Jesse grabbed the wide tape over her mouth and ripped it away. *Oooww!* Her eyes watered. The pain was excruciating. *Jesse, don't ever try waxing, even if you're as hairy as a goat.*

Open, shut, open, shut – she exercised her stiff jaw. Now her teeth were free to work properly. Like a ravenous animal, she tore at the tape binding her wrists together. It gave way. She used her fingers to tear the tape from the opposite wrist. It was only a few seconds till her ankles were also free. The tape stuck to her fingers. *That might be useful later.* She rolled the strips into sticky balls and put them in her jeans pocket.

Jesse stood and shook her arms and legs. They tingled a little but worked just fine. *So far, so good. Now, how do I get out of here?* A careful check of each wall showed no windows, chutes or trapdoors. Her shoulder bag was not here. Any gadgets that might help her had gone along with it. Despite tae kwon do and karate, Jesse knew she couldn't fight her way out of here alone. She wasn't strong enough. *But I have a good brain, better than most. I can use that.*

She looked at her special wristwatch. The face was broken and it rattled. *Useless.*

One hand on her chin, she considered her small prison. Why were there no windows? Was this a storage room? There wasn't much in here if it was. Then she remembered Director Granger's office. That, too, had no windows. Why? It was underground. A flash of inspiration swept through her. If she was below ground, there was only one direction to escape. Up.

34

Feet balanced on the arm of the couch, Jesse stretched above her head to reach the ventilation shaft cover. Using the metal clip from her hair she loosened the two screws that held the cover in place. She held the first screw between her lips while she undid the second. *Faster. There can't be much time left before they check on me.*

Firmly, she tucked the cover into the waist of her jeans, placed both hands on each side of the duct opening and hauled herself upwards. For the first time, she was glad she worked out in the C2 gymnasium.

The shaft was a long silver tube that snaked up into the distance. She couldn't redo the screws from inside. But if the cover was back in place it would take her captors a few minutes longer to work out where she had gone. It might make the difference between escape and capture. She extracted the tape from her pocket and stuck several strips to the sides of the ventilation cover. *It'll have to do.*

Jesse felt a sickness deep in her stomach. She loathed enclosed spaces. But if she sat here, frozen with fear, that would be the end of her.

The shaft swung as she moved. Bracing her body by using her feet, back and hands, she edged upwards. *Just as well this shaft tilts sideways and up, rather than straight up. Otherwise, my arms would drop off.*

Soon the shaft levelled out more. Slowly, wriggling on her stomach like an earthworm, she advanced. She wasn't sure where this would take her, but it was her only option. *If this building is out in the country, I'll be totally lost.*

Then she heard the sound of voices – muffled, male and nearby.

It's OK, just another vent. I'd better be careful or they'll hear me crawling past. She peered down to the room below.

There was another face she knew. Mr Carrillo sat on a stool.

Jesse had a clear view of the top of his head. *He's going bald. Good. He deserves it.*

A man in a white coat bent over Carrillo's extended arm. "What happened, Al?"

"Hit by a tennis ball. It didn't bother me then. But it's still weeping."

The man in the coat lifted a flap of skin on Carrillo's arm and prodded with some kind of instrument.

Gross. What is he doing?

"It's red. Don't want it to become infected. I'll give you something for it. But the connection to the mainframe is still working.".

Mainframe? That's a computer connection in his arm. He's into cybernetics. She had read about people who had terminals inserted surgically in their bodies. They could open doors, read emails, and know what others connected were feeling.

"How's the neck?" The man lifted Mr Carrillo's hair and inspected the back of his neck.

"Working fine."

"Good. And the girl?"

Does he mean me?

"Eva says she's OK. But the procedure is best done tomorrow. Let her rest."

Carrillo rubbed his hands together. "Do you understand what this means? A cybernetically enhanced genius. A marriage of genes and technology. She could be of tremendous use to us here at Cybervision."

No way. I'm not having bits of machinery stuck into my flesh. Gross.

"And C2?"

Good question. And how did he know I was a

genius? It's top secret.

Carrillo puffed his lips in a gesture of contempt. "They don't suspect me. Why should they? I'm their best deep cover agent. I'm just the best for two different sides." He chuckled. "C2 is falling behind the times. Cybernetics is the way of the future and those who realise that will be the leaders of a new society. The implant gives me eyes in the space station, ears in the most secret submarine. It gives me an endless supply of information. Once I learn how to control the implant properly, I can manipulate machinery and information with just my mind. Think about the possibilities."

The man in the white coat nodded as though he had heard all of this before, and agreed.

"It's all worked out rather well. Who else would they send to guard a child? Another child of course. It was the perfect lure to get the kid outside of the building."

"And Jasmine?"

Yes, what about her? It hurt to think Jasmine might have been pretending to like her, to get close, then betray her. A twinge of guilt stung Jesse. That was similar to what she had tried to do. Except her intention had been to save Jasmine, not to hurt her.

"She knows nothing. She should be at the airport, on her way to London."

Relief surged through Jesse.

The door below burst open. Hair dishevelled, face tight with tension, Eva shouted, "The girl's disappeared!"

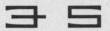

Jesse flinched. She'd heard enough. It was urgent to get out. She wriggled past the vent and further into the shaft. It wouldn't take them long to figure out where she was. But she still had a head start.

She passed two more vents over empty rooms, then stopped when she reached the third. A man lay on the floor. It was Tom, the head of Carrillo security. By the angle of his neck and the stillness of his body, she could tell he was dead.

These people don't muck around. Jesse's heart thumped. She edged along the shaft as fast as she could. Dust danced in the silver shaft, making her nose itch. *If I sneeze over a vent, I'll give myself away.* She pinched the end of her nose and waited for the urge to pass.

She was in big trouble, and not just because she was trapped in a ventilation shaft with maniacs below. Even if she escaped, it would not be over. Those Cybervision people would still know who she was and would try again to catch her. Either to turn her into a partial machine or to silence her.

Seconds later, she crawled over a vent that opened into a room that housed a bank of computers. *This is the mainframe, the brain.* A wild thought flashed through her mind.

The screws for the vent cover were on the outside. *I can kick it open. But when it falls, they'll hear it.* Jesse considered her options for a few seconds, then slid the belt from her jeans and fastened one end around the cover grating. Three hard kicks released the cover. It dangled harmlessly, and silently, from her belt.

Jesse dropped, catlike, to her feet and placed the cover on a chair. She made sure both doors were deadlocked and dragged a table in front of each. *That should give me a few minutes.* Shouting and running feet told her that was about all she had left.

Jesse sat at the computer terminal with a rising sense of panic. Nothing she tried had worked.

A knock sounded at the door. "Who's in there? Let me in."

It was Eva.

No way, not even if you huff and puff.

Jesse rested her head in her hands. What else could she try? She sighed and looked again at the screen. There was only one option left. The cyber implant specifications were on the screen in front of her. They were definitely all connected to this one big computer system. Like drones. Their strength was also their weakness.

Did Carrillo tell them what to do via the computer links? Could he force them, brainwash them? She didn't know. But certainly, they were all aware of each other, like ants before rain. Communicating without sound. Any other time, she would have been fascinated. Right now, she was desperate to stop them.

"The door's locked from the inside, Al," came Eva's voice. "Could she be in there, do you think?"

There was a loud bang as though something heavy was being aimed at the door.

"Blow it up if you have to," came Carrillo's voice.

What happened to Mr Smiling Dad?

He bellowed again, "She must be using the ventilation shaft. Someone get up there. Now! And have security at exit points."

Again, Jesse hoped Jasmine was not a cyber girl.

Her fingers flew over the keyboard. *What do computer nerds always worry about? Viruses. If this mainframe got sick, everything and anyone joined to it would become infected. The connection should be broken.* Grateful for her photographic memory, Jesse typed in one last command, then hesitated. But she had no choice. She hit "enter'. The light in the ceiling flashed and zig-zags shot across the screen, followed by an electrical hiss.

Someone outside the room gave a short scream, then there was silence. A single cursor flashed off and on against the blank computer screen. *That's it. Scrambled, like a carton of eggs.* Jesse hoped the power surge had blown all the circuits, including those embedded in human flesh.

Jesse dragged a chair under the hole in the ceiling and climbed back up into the ventilation shaft. Again, her skin crawled at the idea of being so closed in. She swallowed her fear and forced herself to go on.

She checked in the next room, where the pounding had originated. Below her, Eva and Mr Carrillo wandered in little circles as if they didn't know what they were doing. Their faces were blank, like windup toys.

There was no time to feel sorry for them. Jesse was still in danger. Some of these people might not have implants. As fast as she dared, she headed onward again and came to a dead end. Well, almost a dead end. The shaft went upwards at a sharp angle.

Jesse wanted to cry from frustration. Her lips felt twice their normal size and still stung from the sticky tape, her wrists were red raw and she was tired.

Then she thought about Jai. What would happen to him if she didn't return? He was smart but he wasn't strong emotionally. He needed her. And what about Rohan? Who would search for him if she couldn't? No, she had to get out.

Teeth gritted with determination, Jesse began her ascent. Using her feet to lever her body upwards and her back to steady and balance her against the opposite wall, she inched upwards. Her breath came in tired puffs. Her legs trembled. The silver shaft trembled along with them. Its movement made her queasy.

Aah. She slipped. The sweat on her hands made it difficult to brace herself.

She had no notion of time, just pushed upward, bracing herself for rest every so often. *This isn't as bad as some of the laboratory experiments at C2 and I survived them.*

Suddenly, shockingly, the ventilation shaft evened out again. Jesse slumped, breathing deeply, relieved to have the pressure gone from her legs. *They'll ache tomorrow. If there is a tomorrow.*

When she caught her breath, she edged forward to another vent and looked down. The room below her was familiar. Jesse stifled a giggle, worried she wouldn't be able to stop.

37

"Hello!" Liam stood in the doorway to Jesse's room at C2, a paper bag in his hand. The door was open, ready for Jai's visit.

"Come in," said Jesse.

Liam followed the blue footprints around to a chair at the table and sat. As usual, his blond hair stuck out crazily.

He looked at Jesse's face intently. "How are you?"

"All right."

"I brought you a hamburger." He placed the bag on the table. "Don't tell that Mary woman. She'll have me executed."

Her mouth watered instantly. "Thanks."

"What you did back at the Carrillo house … it was gutsy. Of course, I could have done better." He raised one eyebrow. "But you did all right for a thumb sucker."

Jesse tucked her knees up on the chair and wrapped

her arms around them. "I got a shock when I looked down and saw I was still in the Carrillos" house, over the dining room. I had to stop myself from laughing. I think if I'd started, I would never have stopped."

"Nervous reaction."

"I think I hate the colour apricot now."

"Yeah. Too fruity," said Liam. "I'm not fond of anything that's good for me."

"Thanks for ... rescuing me."

"I didn't. You rescued yourself. All I had to do was drive you back here while the team swept in to remove a few security guards." Liam shrugged. "The zombies were no trouble."

"How are they ... the Cybervision people?"

"Alive and physically well. But no memories. You blew their fuses. Clever. I guess there are advantages to working with a midget genius."

"I'm not a midget," she said. "I'm average height for my age."

"Do you have to argue with everything?"

"Pretty much."

"Director Granger is…" Liam's lips formed an impolite word, then he changed it mid-sentence. "He didn't suspect Carrillo was a double agent. Me? I didn't know he was even supposed to be one of ours. Under deep cover, only Granger and a couple of others knew.

If they'd told us, it might have been different. But they can't work that way. Honesty is too hard an idea for them to grasp."

Jesse nodded.

"I've been given a new assignment," he said.

So that's why he's here, to say goodbye. Another person leaving my life.

"I've been asked to pick a partner … what are you doing next week?"

"Me?"

He looked around the room. "I don't see anyone else in here, unless they're invisible."

"I suppose it's OK." Actually it was perfect. She could get away from here for a few days. The more successful she was in her assignments, the more the Director would trust her. She could search for Rohan and a way to freedom. Maybe even find out about their real families. It would take time, but she would do it.

"I was also hoping you would karate Hans again for me. He's got an attitude."

"You mean he beats you."

"Something like that." Liam drew an envelope from his jacket pocket. "You've got mail."

"Me?"

"That your favourite word today?"

"But I don't know anyone."

"A letter was sent from London to the school you attended. The sender's initials are J.C."

Jasmine Carrillo.

"Prov kind of forgot to pass it on to Granger. I read it. Sorry, but I had to make sure it was OK. You know, no letter bomb or poisoned glue. If you're smart, you won't answer. It's too dangerous to form attachments from assignments. And although she seems innocent herself, she was involved with some nasty people. Be happy she remembers you and move on."

He was right, of course. Jesse stared at the envelope. *My first letter.* She took it, but didn't open it. Later, when she was alone, she'd read it.

"Tell me about our next assignment."

Hello

I've snuck out from C2 for a little while and my friend, Christine Harris, has now set up two email addresses for me.

jesse@christineharris.com

jesse@christineharris.com.au

Any secret communications should be safe on these addresses. I hope lots of readers will write to me after they read my books.

Jesse Sharpe, child prodigy and hamburger lover

Now that you have finished reading Girl Undercover #1, *Secrets*, here is Chapter 1 of Girl Undercover #2, *Fugitive*...

1

Jesse ran. The narrow path twisted around trees and boulders. Her sneakers snapped twigs and scattered fallen leaves. Low-hanging branches slapped her face and ripped at her hair.

Behind her, a dog barked, setting off the whole pack. She pictured them straining at their leashes, mouths curled back from sharp teeth, drooling. She checked her watch. Ten of her fifteen minutes" head start had gone.

Once, she had longed to run outdoors with the wind in her face. But not like this. Not trying to keep ahead of dogs that were trained to hunt. *They go for the throat first.* Unconsciously, Jesse flung one hand up to touch the soft skin of her neck.

She couldn't escape by leaving the path and going cross-country. Out there were high electric fences topped with razor wire. *What if I climb a tree?* she thought. *No, they'd still find me. And I'd have to come down sometime. The dogs would just wait.* The only way to survive was to keep moving forward.

Mouth dry, heart pounding, she burst into a clearing. There was a lake in front of her, straddled by an arched bridge. *Over the bridge or through the water?*

Jesse blinked and craned her head forward. The bridge rails seemed to be squirming. A short dash brought her close enough to be sure. The hairs on her arms stood up as she realised what she was looking at.

CHRISTINE HARRIS

Girl Undercover is Jesse Sharpe. Jesse is twelve years old. She is a prodigy, a genius. She speaks five languages and was reading encyclopedias at age three. With other child prodigies she has been "adopted" by a secret organization, C2, and is on assignment as part of Operation IQ. Children can go where adults cannot, and adults seldom notice them. But that doesn't make Jesse's task any less dangerous…

Girl Undercover #1 Secrets
Girl Undercover #2 Fugitive
Girl Undercover #3 Nightmare
Girl Undercover #4 Danger

Christine Harris is one of Australia's busiest and most popular children's authors. She has written more than thirty books as well as plays, articles, poetry and short stories. Her work has been published in the UK, USA, France and New Zealand.
www.christineharris.com